THE EDGE OF T

Taking up the story of *Flambards* opens on the winter morning wh Aunt Grace's London house in a Rolls-Royce and wearing a pink ball-dress. She and her cousin Will have run away together like a pair of fairy-tale lovers.

But Will's passionate ambition to design, make, and fly aeroplanes is a hard one to realize. So many people are caught up in the new craze that jobs are scarce, he has no money to buy materials, and his stiff leg is a dreadful handicap in managing the machines.

Christina too has battles to win: getting a job at a time when the idea of a young girl working for her living is frowned upon, learning to control the terror she feels every time Will is in the air, and even to face flying herself. Hardest of all, she has to come to terms with the truth that Will's love for her is of a different kind from his dedicated passion for aeroplanes, and that in a way she must always take second place.

This second book in the Flambards series was awarded the Carnegie Medal.

Kathleen Peyton grew up in the London suburbs and always longed to live in the country and have a horse. Although she wrote stories for her own entertainment and had her first book published when she was fifteen, she always wanted to be a painter, and when she left school went to Kingston Art School and later, when her family moved, to Manchester Art School. Here she met her husband, Michael, a graphics artist and cartoonist. They have worked together all their lives, choosing to live in Essex in order to be near good sailing, and to London. They have two daughters.

And since she has made some money from publishing her books, Kathleen has always had a horse, or several.

Other Oxford Children's Modern Classics

The Eagle of the Ninth
Rosemary Sutcliff

Outcast
Rosemary Sutcliff

The Silver Branch
Rosemary Sutcliff

The Lantern Bearers
Rosemary Sutcliff

Minnow on the Say
Philippa Pearce

Tom's Midnight Garden
Philippa Pearce

The Ship That Flew
Hilda Lewis

A Little Lower than the Angels
Geraldine McCaughrean

A Pack of Lies
Geraldine McCaughrean

Brother in the Land
Robert Swindells

Flambards
K. M. Peyton

Wolf
Gillian Cross

The Great Elephant Chase
Gillian Cross

The Hounds of the Morrigan
Pat O'Shea

K. M. PEYTON

The Edge
of the Cloud

Illustrated by Victor G. Ambrus

OXFORD UNIVERSITY PRESS
Oxford   New York   Toronto

Oxford University Press, Great Clarendon Street, Oxford OX2 6DP

Oxford New York
Athens Auckland Bangkok Bogota Buenos Aires Calcutta
Cape Town Chennai Dar es Salaam Delhi Florence Hong Kong Istanbul Karachi
Kuala Lumpur Madrid Melbourne Mexico City Mumbai
Nairobi Paris Sao Paulo Singapore Taipei Tokyo Toronto Warsaw

and associated companies in
Berlin Ibadan

Oxford is a trade mark of Oxford University Press

First published 1969
Reprinted 1972, 1987

First published in this edition 1998

British Library Cataloguing in Publication Data
Data available

Cover illustration by Angelo Rinaldi

ISBN 0 19 271782 0

Printed and bound in Great Britain by
Biddles Ltd, Guildford and King's Lynn

TO
VERONICA

CHAPTER I

'We've eloped,' Christina said to Aunt Grace. She had not meant
to use the silly word, but it had got stuck in her head, and she was
too befuddled with cold to catch it before it slipped out.

Aunt Grace, standing in her dressing-gown on her Battersea
doorstep, was understandably astonished. She had last seen Christina five years ago, when the child had been twelve, and William
when he was a baby. The Rolls-Royce, parked beside the kerb,
was no less a source of wonder.

'Is that motor-car yours?' she said to William.

'I borrowed it,' William said apologetically.

'You've driven up from Flambards in it?'

'Yes.'

'You must be mad,' Aunt Grace said. 'And frozen to death. Come in, you silly children.'

It had been just past midnight when they had started out, skimming through the dark countryside, keyed up with love and excitement so that progress was like some mythical flight, all fire and gold, the motor a chariot and they immortal . . . but now dawn showed a streaked sky and the factory chimneys were putting out streamers of smoke, the only banners of welcome; the cobbles were grey and greasy, the brick houses dingy, pointed with soot. Christina did not want to look. Real life was taking over too fast as it was. She was so cold that the clammy, gas-smelling embrace of Aunt Grace's hall was almost welcoming.

'The fires aren't lit yet, only in the kitchen. Go through, dear. It's nice and warm in there and I'll make you some breakfast.'

The shiny linoleum, and the wallpaper with blue peacocks on it were completely familiar to Christina, as if she had never been away. William was right to have chosen Aunt Grace for refuge. Although surprised, she was entirely practical. Her life was in order, her house clean and neat, her advice would be to the point. Christina had no doubt that they were going to receive much advice before they were through. She looked at William, and he smiled at her, as if he was not worried at all. He looked very odd, with a white clean patch round his eyes where the goggles had been, and the rest of his face all grimy. Christina went on looking at him, amazed by what they had done.

'Now tell me what this is all about,' Aunt Grace said. 'I hope you haven't been very silly. Sit by the fire there. Get thawed out. The kettle won't take a moment.'

She was at work already, laying cups and saucers on the scrubbed kitchen table. The kitchen was small, scrupulously tidy, and the range gave out a gorgeous warmth, burnishing the blackleading with a rosy glow. The kettle purred over the bars. Christina curled herself over the heat, opening her coat so that the crystal beads on her ball-dress winked and glittered.

Five years ago she had lived in this house. The fire was an embrace, unlocking tiny set-pieces of memory: crumpets in the sitting-room, when she was twelve, flames lighting spark patterns

2

on the soot of the chimney back, and herself trying to tell her own fortune in them. Ever since the age of five, when her parents had been killed, she had been anxious—understandably—as to what was to become of her, and had looked for her fortune in every teacup, and every fireback. She had received scant comfort, shuttled from relative to relative, before coming to Aunt Grace, where she would have happily stayed. But family politics had decided otherwise.

'I hope,' Aunt Grace was saying, with a slight severity, 'that you have not lost your sense of responsibility. Your Uncle Russell has given you a home for the last five years: you owe him a great deal. I would have thought that his two boys would have become more like brothers to you in that length of time, than prospective husbands.'

'Only Will is a prospective husband, Aunt Grace.'

'The trouble was,' William put in, 'we both wanted her. But Mark, because he's the oldest, assumed she was going to marry him, and when she said she didn't want to, Mark was so furious that we decided to come away.'

'You may have been brought up in the country,' Aunt Grace said, 'but there is no need to talk like a farmer. You both *wanted* her, indeed! Elevate yourself from the level of the stockyard, William, and tell me how you intend to support Christina in the married state.'

Will smiled, unabashed.

'I shall get a job, Aunt Grace.'

'In what profession?'

'Flying.'

'Oh, good grief!' Aunt Grace was visibly shaken. She stared at William, seeing a tall, thin boy of eighteen with black hair and dark, intelligent eyes. He had a stiff leg, locked at the knee, yet moved with a remarkable rolling ease. She knew that he was phenomenally clever, unlike his brother Mark, and his obsession with flying-machines was not news to her. She knew he could fly, this curious, gangling boy: a rare accomplishment in this year of grace, nineteen hundred and twelve. But this was no recommendation when it came to thinking of a husband, the reverse if

3

anything: flying was a shockingly dangerous sport. And eighteen! Aunt Grace pursed her lips.

'You're very young to be thinking of marriage, the two of you.' She shook some tea into the teapot.

'Oh, we know it will be years yet. Will has to work things out,' Christina said. 'We have no plans, but you understand why we had to come away?'

'Because Mark asked you to marry him, you refused, he was furious—that is in character, as I remember Mark—and your further presence under the same roof threatened to be embarrassing? Yes, I understand. But why Will?'

'Why Will what, Aunt Grace?'

Did she not understand that they were in love? Christina looked up at her aunt, who had not loved for very many years, her husband having been run down by a horse-bus. Will, sensing Christina's mutiny, said hastily, 'But my father has thrown me out already, Aunt Grace. I left home two weeks ago. I only went back to take Christina to the Hunt Ball.'

'And why did Russell throw you out, may I ask?'

'Because he disapproves of my flying. He arranged to send me to British Columbia, so I left home.'

'Oh. And where have you been living since you left home?' Aunt Grace asked William.

'Around the aircraft sheds at Brooklands, and Eastchurch and that, looking for a job.'

'You've got one?'

'No. But I've got an interview at Farnborough on Monday.'

'Hmm.' Aunt Grace, having marshalled most of the relevant facts, poured out three cups of tea and cut some bread to make toast. Christina, basking over the fire, threw back her coat and straightened up to reach for her tea. Aunt Grace, glancing at the bare, white shoulders, the arms hard with holding the strength of her Uncle Russell's hunters, the hair tumbling in a thick brown tangle over the nape of her neck, was not surprised at the desires of the Russell boys. Christina was no conventional beauty: she was too firm and strong and straight. Looking at her, Aunt Grace could well believe that she was a fine horsewoman, in the Russell

4

tradition—her occasional letters had been full of horse news and hunting tales. She could well believe too, looking at her stubborn mouth and slightly wary eyes, that Christina was used to working out her own salvation. At Flambards, no doubt, she had no option. She had never known a mother, or comfort, in the ordinary sense. She had learned to look after herself. Aunt Grace liked Christina, basically. She was in the Russell mould, after her mother. Aunt Grace did not want things to go wrong for Christina.

'I've no doubt,' she said, 'everything will work itself out. It all depends upon yourselves. I think you need some sleep, before you start making plans. And some boiled eggs.'

They had known Aunt Grace was sensible. They had been right to rely on her. Christina found it hard to believe, knowing Aunt Grace in her Battersea setting, that she had been a girl at Flambards, and had hunted the corn-fed hunters over the same Essex fields as herself, that she knew the park and the chestnut trees and the rookery and the over-grown pink roses just as she knew them herself. Christina was so tired that the roses and the horses and the boiled eggs all went round together in front of her eyes. Almost immediately, it seemed, she was being tucked into bed with a hot bottle for company. The sheets were stiff and clean as no Flambards sheets had been for years, the mattress feathers soft, lapping her like a swan its ducklings. Christina slept, oblivious of her new love and life.

Aunt Grace, having already slept, was by no means as oblivious. She sat in the kitchen, stirring her cup of tea (after dispatching William to drive his Rolls-Royce up to the bus stables and get it locked in a cart shed—Aunt Grace knew the little boys of Battersea). She was a resilient woman, very hard and at the same time very human; this sudden predicament of her brother's son and her sister's daughter both worried her, and touched her. Marriage, at their age! She did not think either of them knew what love was about; yet—knowing her brother Russell's tyrannical nature—she could well understand their running away to work out a solution of their own. One could scarcely work out so delicate a relationship in the charged atmosphere of Russell's disapproval. Russell was a violent man when crossed, and Aunt Grace knew that

Russell had intended Christina to marry Mark, not William. Mark was his favourite, a handsome, ignorant, hard-riding boy who was in both looks and temperament the image of his father. Mark was to inherit Flambards, and carry on the stables, whose hunters were second to none in Essex, and to do this he needed money. Christina, when she was twenty-one, would have money, having been left a considerable amount by her father. Aunt Grace knew that it was to this end alone that Russell had demanded that Christina be brought up at Flambards. Living in a bygone age, he was still of the opinion that young people married whoever was allotted them, and he had arranged that Christina would marry Mark.

Aunt Grace smiled with a somewhat feline satisfaction. No doubt all was not peace in the Flambards household this morning. She was only relieved that Russell's physical state—for he had been crippled in a hunting accident—assured that he would not arrive in pursuit on her doorstep.

'So,' she said to William, when he returned, 'you have set yourself some problems. I hope you know what you're doing.'

'Yes, Aunt Grace. If only Christina can stay here until I get a job and earn some money—it won't be long—then we shall be all right.'

'They'll give you a job, with that stiff leg of yours?'

William's expression changed. 'It makes no difference,' he said shortly.

'Hmm.' Aunt Grace's bluntness was no surprise to William, for he had heard of it from Christina, but his expression darkened still further when she said, 'You're not after Christina's money?'

'By the time she comes into her money I shall have made plenty of money of my own,' he said stiffly.

'Don't take offence, silly boy. I'm only your aunt. I'm entitled to ask questions like that. Surely money is a subject of perennial interest?'

'Yes. Yes, of course.' William had to admit the truth of her remark. He had two sovereigns in his pocket, and would have no more till he earned some. During the last two weeks he had known hunger for the first time in his life.

'You need some sleep.' Aunt Grace got up from the table.

'There's a bed in my sewing-room. I shan't be working in there this morning. Come along. I'll show you.'

And William was pleased to feel that, for the next few hours, there would be no need to think.

Christina awoke at four in the afternoon, heavy with dreams of Flambards. The wind and rain were blowing about the black branches of the chestnut-trees and bending the dead yellow grass in the park; the wind was in the horses' tails, and in their demeanour, so that they kept skipping and joggling and reaching out with impatience . . . She opened her eyes and saw the rain running down the sooty window glass. 'Will! Oh, Will!' she cried out, and stretched out her arms as if she expected to find him lying beside her. But the sheets beyond the little cave of her body warmth were bare and cold, and she remembered that she had not so much as kissed him yet, and this was Battersea. Here the horses were in coster carts and the chestnuts behind park palisades. Will was drinking tea in the kitchen with Aunt Grace. 'No, it's late,' she thought. The wet sky had a wedge of pink sunset in it, tremulous and tear-stained. The clouds were ragged with wind . . . no wonder the horses were so wild . . .

Christina raised herself up on her elbows and shook back the weight of her hair. She looked again at the rain on the window, and saw that there was no beauty in it. She was awake now, remembering what she had done. There were no horses.

She looked round cautiously. This was the room she had slept in when she was twelve, a high, narrow room with a big brass bed and a marble-topped washstand, and cold linoleum on the floor. There was only one chair, and over it her lovely pink ball-dress, the only dress she now possessed. The night of the ball seemed ten years ago. 'Yet this time yesterday,' she thought, 'I hadn't even started dressing for it. I didn't even know if Will would come.' Certainly she had never guessed that they would run away from the ball together like fairy-tale lovers. It was very hard, now, to remember how it had come about, very hard to recall that mixture of delirious, swooning excitement and needle-sharp fear, the atmosphere of champagne and camellias, and the scrunching of

7

the motor wheels on the gravel. 'But it happened,' she said to herself, 'or I wouldn't be here now.'

Lying in bed, she felt now very different from how she had felt last night. 'It's the smell of polish, and gasometers,' she thought. But she knew now that she was afraid of what she had done, not afraid of loving Will, but of having turned herself out of Flambards, which was the only real home she had ever known. She had nothing, now. Only Aunt Grace's charity. She could not get out of bed, because she did not even have a dress to wear for everyday.

'I shall have to get a job, like Will,' she thought. But the only thing she could do well was ride a horse. 'Aunt Grace will make me sew,' she thought, for Aunt Grace was a dressmaker by trade, and Christina remembered how she had sewed when she was twelve, hour after hour in the morning-room downstairs, listening to the putter of the gas and the horses' hooves clopping slackly on the road outside, and the coal falling in the grate. Thinking of it, she tried not to shiver a little. Her hands were coarse with holding Uncle Russell's horses. She was used to the wet fields and the mud flying, and the rain in her face.

'Oh, you're awake. Good.' Aunt Grace's face appeared round the door. 'I've been looking out some clothes for you. I think these will do.' From an armful which consisted mostly of sensible drawers and camisoles and petticoats she shook out a fawn crêpe blouse with a high neck and buttoned cuffs, and a long, dark-brown serge walking skirt.

'I'll fetch you a jug of hot water, dear.' She laid the clothes out on the chair.

'Is Will up?'

'He was up an hour ago, dear. I gave him a meal and he left about ten minutes ago.'

Christina shot up in bed. 'Left!'

'Yes, dear.'

'Where's he gone?'

'To Farnborough, he said. His appointment is in the morning, and he said he'd rather be there the night before, just in case he had trouble with the motor-car.'

'Oh!' Christina's voice was almost a wail. 'He—oh, I'd forgotten—of course, it's Sunday now. Oh, I wish he'd said good-bye!'

'I looked in, dear, but you were asleep.' Aunt Grace disappeared, and Christina threw herself back into the pillows and moaned softly to herself, 'Oh, Will, I want you here!' It was only because he had gone away, in the first place, that she had discovered that she loved him. At least, knowing little of love, she supposed that the pain of the parting meant that she was in love. This pain, compounded of frustration and loneliness, shot through with nerve-flicking stabs of doubt and seamed with chasms of confusion, had dogged her for the whole fortnight before the ball, and was so familiar to her that she recognized the symptoms of its recurrence immediately. She wanted to cry with disappointment. Where was romance now, in the cold house of her great-aunt? Her eyes fell bitterly on the sensible underwear and the sombre skirt. The ball-dress had fallen off the chair out of sight, as if quenched by the stark uniform of everyday. It symbolized exactly Christina's feelings.

But no one, Christina knew—as she lay back staring at the grey ceiling—was going to make things any different for her. She had been brave last night, running away, because it had been easy. But now, in the wet spring dusk of a Battersea Sunday evening, she needed courage, and there was none in her. Her mind was full of her dreams of Flambards and, just as she had loved William when he had gone away, so now with a capriciousness that enraged her she found herself feeling desperately homesick.

'You're mad!' she said to herself. 'You don't know what you want! You never loved Flambards when you were there!'

But this ache was something compounded of every love and every pain she had ever remotely known; it was a homesickness for something she did not even know.

'Here's the water, dear. When you're ready there's a nice tea waiting.'

Christina felt that Aunt Grace was glad that William had gone, and that the two of them were cosily together, like old times. She was not used to men. 'Nor am I,' Christina thought, 'not in this new way.' She steeled herself to get out of bed, not to cry. Her warm feet flinched on the linoleum, like the feel of a horse going

9

to refuse. 'Horses have courage,' Christina thought. 'They have to do whatever is asked of them, however hard.' She would have to be a horse. She had stopped the threat of tears now. She could face the serge skirt and the drab blouse. Aunt Grace was kind. If there had been no Aunt Grace, then she would have had cause to be afraid. By the time she had dressed she had found what she supposed was courage, a sort of numb resignation. (She had seen that in horses too.) She thought of Will, driving through the dusk with the awkwardness of his leg making him swear, his head full of his aeroplane dreams, and went down to tea with Aunt Grace. The velour curtains were drawn. There was toast on the brass tripod in front of the fire, and seedcake in slices. The room was very small, after Flambards, but warm, with none of Flambards' whistling draughts. There was a thick curtain on a brass rail over the door, and a velvet sausage hanging on a cord over the keyhole, and another at the foot of the door. Christina felt sealed in, a prisoner amongst the bric-à-brac of Aunt Grace's possessions. The only way out was with the flames up the chimney. Aunt Grace, having had all day to consider the significance of the events, seemed at ease.

'Perhaps it will be as well that you've left Flambards,' she said. 'A young girl needs to see a little city life. There is plenty here for you to do, and I shall enjoy your company. You will have to write to Russell and smooth him over. There is no need to mention Will. After all, you're much too young to be engaged, especially as Will has no prospects.'

'I only came away to be with Will,' Christina said, all the agony coming back with a rush. 'I—'

'Will has to make his way. He will not do it overnight. You must have patience, Christina. After all, you cannot get married without Russell's permission until you are both twenty-one, and I cannot see him giving it. And Will has chosen a very precarious career . . . however did he come to get interested in flying?'

'A man at home—a neighbour—has built an aeroplane, and Will helped him, and flew it for him. Mr. Dermot—' Christina tried not to choke on the memory of Mr. Dermot, who was more of a father to Will than his own had ever been. 'When Uncle

Russell found out about Mr. Dermot, he said Will must go to British Columbia, to some relation—he forbade him to see Mr. Dermot again. He said he would prosecute Mr. Dermot otherwise. So Will left home.'

'How can Will fly an aeroplane when he has a stiff leg?'

'He flew Mr. Dermot's all right.'

'He ought to see a doctor. It could very possibly be put right.'

'They said it would never be right again.' Christina felt the room closing in on her again. Aunt Grace's brisk words did not allow for dreams. She felt stifled.

'Have some toast,' Aunt Grace ordered.

When the tea was finished and cleared away, Aunt Grace got out a workbox and started to sew. After half an hour she suggested to the silent Christina that she might like to help with some lace insertions, and in another five minutes Christina was sewing too. She bent her head very low over the work, and her whole being cried out, 'I can't bear it! I can't bear it!' But she said nothing, and sewed until it was time for bed.

Chapter 2

'A cup of tea and a cheese sandwich, please.' William gave his order to the waitress, trying to keep his eyes off a large plateful of sausage rolls she had in her hand, hot from the oven. He could have eaten the lot with no trouble at all.

'I don't think I can bear many more days like this,' he thought. This was the fourth time he had come to this table, in order to sit and stare out over the cold, short grass of Elm Park flying-field. The café was just inside the gates into the field, and catered largely for the spectators, mechanics, pupils, and instructors that made up the local population. Its steamy atmosphere, laced with purely technical conversation, was both bliss and torture to William. He was drawn to it like a homing pigeon to its loft, yet, once arrived, it was as if the loft door was shut and he was on the perch outside, only able to watch the other fat, contented pigeons through the wire mesh.

It was three weeks since he had left Battersea for his interview at Farnborough. This interview had been the first of many, but still, in William's mind, the most hurtful and discouraging—probably because, in those distant, golden days, he was still full of what he had thought was unshakable confidence. And it seemed to William a year ago, not a mere three weeks, that he had felt confident in his own ability. Before the Farnborough interview he had considered himself sound in wind and limb, an able pilot, a good engineer, and a promising designer. But since the interview he had discovered that—having no Aero Club ticket of proficiency—he could not be considered a pilot, that mechanics could only be proficient if they had a mass of references to back up their word and that—cruellest cut of all—his leg put him in the category of 'cripple'. The man at Farnborough had been kind, brief, and adamant. William had explained, 'It's designing I want to do most of all. That's why I came to Farnborough first', but the man had not been interested in his parcel of drawings. 'We are always keen to see new designs. You fly it here, and we'll look at it.' But William's aeroplane was still on paper. 'I'm sorry,' the man concluded, 'but every day we are asked to employ this or that brilliant designer, half a dozen brilliant test pilots and batches of inspired mechanics. Yes, we are interested in new ideas, but we want to see them working, not on paper. You go and build your aeroplane, and you can fly it in our competition in August. That is the way to get Farnborough interested in you.'

'I've no money,' William said simply.

'No,' the man said heavily, 'that is the trouble with us all.'

Three weeks later he had even less money. He had three shillings and twopence. He had been back to Essex to return the Rolls-Royce to Mr. Dermot, but had been too proud to tell Mr. Dermot that nobody wanted to employ his skill. He had told him that he was trying to make up his mind between several possible openings, and had come away as soon as was decently possible. Nobody at Farnborough or Brooklands or Hendon had heard of Mr. Dermot. William's one reference, proclaiming his head for mathematics and the science of flight, and his intuitive handling of machines, was scanned without striking a spark in any of its readers. William was told everywhere, 'We are not looking for anybody. We have all the people we want.' And they looked at his leg politely, but did not mention it, only in their eyes.

Having closely watched the antics at the various flying-schools from the spectator stands, William knew that he could fly as well, or better, than most of the instructors. Since Mr. Blériot had flown the Channel three years ago, proving that flying 'worked', the enthusiasts and the money-makers had set up flying-schools with any old bus they could lay their hands on to exploit this flood of flying fever. A few of them, like Bristol's and Sopwith's at Brooklands and Mr. Grahame-White's at Hendon, were efficient and well run, but a lot of them, from William's point of view, flung up in a rackety shed on the corner of one of the same fields, or in some cramped field of its own out in the country, were thoroughly dangerous, with ill-maintained machines and ham-handed pilots. At Elm Park there were three flying-schools housed in the inevitable row of hangars-cum-workshops. Two of them boasted a decrepit Henri Farman pusher biplane each, and one, called the Silver Cloud School of Aviation, actually had two machines, a Henri Farman and a Blériot monoplane. It only had one instructor, though, and William, on the assumption that two aeroplanes warranted two instructors, had already applied to the owner of the school for the vacant post.

'The mechanic has a job to keep one darned aeroplane flying as it is. Why should I want two instructors when I've only ever got one damned machine at a time?' The owner of the Silver Cloud School of Aviation—Percy Adams—was an unattractive man with a dark moustache.

'I could keep both machines flying if you employed me as a mechanic,' William offered promptly.

'Ah, they all say that. You'd want paying, wouldn't you? I'm paying one pilot and one mechanic as it is. I can't pay any more.'

William offered to work for just his meals, but Adams could not even afford to pay for three meals a day. The other two proprietors were equally unwilling and, having offered his services to all the other private aircraft owners on the field and found no joy, William had come to a dead end. He had now spent over a week hanging around Elm Park with a vague hope in the back of his mind that one of the instructors might fall sick or one of the mechanics get a poisoned thumb or something equally inhibiting, but each day had seen him no further forward, merely a little colder, a little hungrier, and a good deal more depressed.

Sitting hour after hour over a cup of tea in the window of the café, he had watched the work-worn Henri Farmans lumbering over the grass, and thought of the small, graceful craft that was on paper in his folio. 'Build your aeroplane,' the man at Farnborough had said, and William knew that he could, if he could earn any money to buy the materials. His confidence had not been shaken on that score. And more than anything in the world he wanted to build his neat biplane. There was still an empty shed in the row with a work-bench at the back and a squat black coal-stove with a rusty chimney, and in this empty shed William dreamed of his biplane taking shape. In the other sheds there were crude machines cosseted by owners who had more money than sense; William had examined them all, and spoken with their owners, and knew that he knew more than all of them. But he had no money.

'I've got about four more days,' he thought, 'before I starve.' His hands closed round the loose coins in his pocket. At night he slept in a barn of hay at the top of the field, and one of the mechanics who kept a Deperdussin monoplane in trim for a wealthy young heir to a baronetcy let him wash and shave with a kettle of hot water at the back of his shed, and share a pan of porridge with him before he started work every morning. 'Four more days, and then—' William stared out of the window—'what, after that?' He was desperately hungry, even after the cheese sandwich.

Coming up the steps of the café was the young man whose job he coveted, Mr. Adams's single instructor. This was the man William was wishing an indisposition on, even a mild crash. He was entirely likeable, hence William's diffidence in wishing him ill. He was a little older than William himself, and spoke with the hint of a Scottish accent. He had an easy, rather quiet manner, untidy sandy-red hair and a faint scattering of freckles on a good-natured but thin, and slightly drawn face. He worked extremely long hours, William had noticed, which accounted for his tired look, and flew rather recklessly when he was on his own, but with great precision when he had a pupil with him. He had his latest pupil with him now. It was—William blinked—a girl. And William could well understand why the teacher thought this pupil was worth treating to a cup of tea, for she was extremely pretty, with thick auburn hair and provocative brown eyes, and a very trim but well-rounded figure which an expensive leather coat set off to advantage. William stared. He did not know girls were learning to fly, let alone girls that looked like this. The pair sat down at the table next to William's, and while the instructor gave the waitress his order the girl looked at William in a bold, appraising way, then dropped her dark red eyelashes with a practised swoop which made him smile. He could not imagine Christina being so obvious. The instructor turned away from the waitress, sent William a friendly nod, and said to the girl, 'You won't be long going solo if you carry on as you did today.'

'Really, Sandy? Do you mean it?'

'Oh, yes. You've got the intuitive—er—thing—that matters.' Sandy gave a vast yawn, apologized, and added, 'I can't think of the right word. I must say, I'm glad there's no one else to take up today.'

'You're glad there was me, though?'

'Oh, of course. I'm sorry. I didn't say the wrong thing, did I? I'm not very smooth with girls—not enough practice, you know.' He smiled, unabashed, and smothered another enormous yawn. 'Excuse me. No reflection on you, you know, just the hours of honest toil, warm atmosphere and all that.'

William could see that Sandy's frank humour was a hit with the girl, whom he had already branded as 'fast'. Her name was Dorothy, he discovered. He tried to turn his attention away from the couple, but could not help wanting to listen. He envied the easy Sandy from the bottom of his heart—but not for the girl. It was the job he envied him for. William knew he could do the job, even if he couldn't flirt with the female pupils—not that this last accomplishment would be much in demand for, as far as William knew, Dorothy was a unique specimen. He stared gloomily out of the window, to where the two-seater Blériot that the pair had been using was being wheeled back to its hangar. The Farman had been out of use for two days, owing to engine trouble, and to William's ears the Blériot's engine sounded in dire need of attention as well. Brought up on Mr. Dermot's standards, William had been shocked to learn how casually many of these aircraft were maintained. As if summoned by William's thoughts, the ineffective mechanic employed by Mr. Adams appeared at the door of the café and made his way over to the instructor's table.

'Begging your pardon, Mr. Hardcastle, sir, but Mr. Adams wants you to take the Farman up before you knock off, to see if it's all right for Mr. Pritchard in the morning.'

'Oh, no!' Sandy Hardcastle half-groaned, half-yawned. 'I'm only flesh and blood! He's had twelve hours out of me today. It'll be all right, surely? You ought to know.'

'Well, I didn't want to say as much to Mr. Adams, sir, but it's still running a bit half-hearted, like. I thought you might be able to put your finger on it if you gave it a trial.'

'I can put my finger on it from here. It's clapped out from over-work, like me. You tell Mr. Adams that.'

The mechanic looked appalled. 'You know I can't do that, sir.'

William, feeling very sick somewhere in his stomach regions, said, 'I'll look at it for you, if you like. I'll give it a trial.'

The three people at the adjoining table turned round and stared at him. William met Sandy's gaze, and knew that he, at least, knew what desperation had prompted the offer. He could also see, quite plainly, that Sandy wanted to stay with the girl, and that he was not averse to taking a gamble. Very tense, he watched Sandy consider the offer. The gamble Sandy was required to take was not a quarter the size of the one he had just proposed for himself.

'I take it you *can* fly?' the instructor said, doubtfully.

'I'd hardly be offering if I couldn't, would I?' William replied.

Sandy grinned. 'I know you're after my job. Well, I'll take a chance and keep Dorothy company a bit longer. I hope you break your darned neck, then I can relax. But don't break the machine up, whatever you do, else we'll all be looking for work.' He shoved the chair holding his woollen muffler, heavy coat, cap and goggles over towards William and said, 'Put these on, then if old Adams looks out of the office window he'll think it's me. You'll need them anyway.'

William stood up and started to pull on the coat. He was too scared by his fortune—whether good or bad was yet to be proved —to say anything.

'Seriously,' Sandy said, 'if she misses a note, get that nose down right away. You know that, don't you?'

'Yes.'

'And she needs right rudder on to fly straight. You'll find that out. One circle of the field will do, just to keep Adams happy. If you do any more he'll suspect something, because he knows what a lazy devil I am.'

The mechanic, looking very worried, stood by William while he gathered up Sandy's gear. Already William's mind was on the problem in hand. He knew the theory, but had never flown a Farman, a very different machine from Mr. Dermot's little *Emma*. He knew, in fact, that it would be much easier to fly than *Emma*, once he had got the hang of it (the whole trouble with *Emma* was that, fast and nippy as she was, she had suicidal habits), but his difficulty would be to get the hang of it instantly, without any preliminary running along the ground or kangaroo-hopping, in order to satisfy the critical gaze of Sandy Hardcastle out of the café windows, and the unsuspecting Mr. Adams, should he be watching. The fact that the machine's engine was suspect was also no great comfort. Even when it was in order it had scarcely enough power to get the clumsy machine over the boundary tree-tops, and William did not like the idea of stalling into the ground in a pusher biplane. At least in *Emma* the engine hit the ground first in the case of a nose-dive, but in the Farman the pilot hit it first and the engine, mounted behind him, merely served to push the pilot farther into the ground. A nasty habit, to William's way of thinking.

Now he was on his feet and about to fly, William, although nervous, felt his confidence flooding back. This was a chance, and up to now he had never been given even that. He followed the mechanic out into the cold, sharp air. The afternoon was pink and still, with only an hour to go to dusk. The Farman waited alone on the grass, like a sinister grasshopper, its two great square-tipped wings throwing a faint shadow. It was two years old and to William's eyes already archaic.

'I reckon she'll fly tail-down, sir. The engine's not giving full power. I thought as how Mr. Hardcastle might be able to tell me why.'

William thought that, if he didn't get Sandy's job, he might well get the inefficient mechanic's. One look at the engine showed him that it was in a filthy condition. He would have liked to have spent some time examining it before flying, but, as he was supposed to be Mr. Hardcastle—for the sake of Mr. Adams looking out of his office window—he thought he had better make his flight straight away. Better to take the risk and prove that he could actually fly, than perhaps never get off the ground at all by getting sidetracked with the engine. One circuit of the aerodrome was all

Sandy had stipulated. He wound the muffler round his neck and tucked the ends in, pulled the cap well on—with the peak at the back—and went round to the front of the machine.

In the Farman the pilot sat virtually on the front of the lower wing with his feet on the rudder-bar which projected a little in front of him. The engine was behind him, and the propeller at the back, pushing rather than pulling. On his right was the lever to control direction; on his left the engine switch and throttle lever. In front of him was nothing at all, save the slender struts carrying the elevator. He was faced with pure sky, riding this invisible mount like a jockey on the ears of his horse. After Mr. Dermot's little craft, where one sat with the wings and engine in sight, William found the Farman extraordinary. He also found that it was impossible to rest his stiff leg on the rudder-bar; it projected some way in front of it.

'Cor blimey, sir, I don't see as 'ow you can fly with a limb like that,' the mechanic said.

He could have found no words better suited to fix William's determination.

'I've never had any trouble before,' he said coldly. This was hardly surprising as on *Emma* he had built himself a specially shaped rudder-bar to cope with the situation, but he was not going to explain this to the mechanic. He would take off and make his circle with the leg that worked, and work out how to cope with this difficulty later on. Some other mechanics had already drifted over to hold on to the tail, and the Farman's own mechanic put on a resigned expression. William switched the petrol on. 'This is it,' he thought.

'Contact!' he called out.

The engine took its time about starting but, once away, its roar was confident enough to comfort William slightly. The familiar smell and noise intoxicated him after his miserable alien weeks on the perimeter of the field. He put up his hand to signal to the mechanics to let go, and sent a little prayer of gratitude in Sandy's direction (and he had no doubt that Sandy was paying for his glib decision, and watching him from the window with sweat on his brow). The old Farman trundled away, wilful as to direction like all machines on the ground, but William managed to get her up into the slight wind without too many deviations and on course for what he hoped would prove a perfect take-off. She roared over the grass.

'Oh, God,' William prayed, 'please make it all go right!' It mattered so much this time.

The wind started to find the gaps in William's hasty dressing, cold and merciless. The ground between his knees was a flattened blur. He eased the stick a fraction to bring up the tail . . . then back, very gently . . . The ground was away, gnashing its cold teeth at the escaping bird. William felt the ecstatic swing in the pit of his stomach which meant that he was in his element again. He glanced to either side along the corridors of swaying struts and screaming flightwires and above him to where the sunset was showing pink on the upper plane, and felt utter, unalloyed bliss. The three weeks of waiting were away with the dull grass and the diminishing sheds.

'Climb, you old pig!' he shouted, and the wing he sat on shuddered with the effort. With full throttle on, she barely cleared the line of trees at the end of the field, and William knew that she was grossly underpowered. But he was not unduly worried. It gave him an excuse for rather more than the mere circuit of the field Sandy had stipulated, for by the time he had gained enough height to make a safe turn he reckoned he would be well out into the country. He thought of Mr. Dermot's little *Emma*, which would be away now above the glowing red ball of the spring sunset, all grace and spit, fickle as a girl with all the defects of her inadequate design. Lovely as she was for her agility, she was unmarketable because of her many deficiencies. Mr. Dermot was forever modifying and rebuilding. William, much as he respected Mr. Dermot, knew that his own version of *Emma*, on paper in his folio, was a far better machine than any Mr. Dermot had yet thought out. 'I shall build her, if I get a job,' he thought. 'She will be a winner!' Oh, this lovely optimism—he had forgotten how it felt! He sat on the wing of the struggling biplane and saw himself hundreds of feet above at the controls of his own little craft, climbing in wide circles like a hawk . . . he wanted to sing . . .

The Gnome motor behind him missed a beat, spat, roared and cut out.

The song died on William's lips. Instantly he pushed the lever forward.

'God in heaven, get me out of this!' he prayed.

The old biplane wobbled perilously. William felt her old-woman mentality wondering whether to stall, or whether to humour her silly pilot by getting her nose down. She rolled a little, uncertain, then answered William's prayer by dropping into a glide. In the horrible silence the wind started to sing in the wires. William peered down between his knees, tense. There was no room at all to manoeuvre, only to get her straight down. A farm roof flashed past with reaching chimneys. There were fields beyond . . . just one hedge to clear with elm-trees to find a way through. 'It will be all right,' William judged—and in the same moment saw the single electric wire strung out on posts across the field. 'Oh, you cursed modern farmer!' he moaned.

The elm-trees loomed, one at each wing-tip. The overgrown hedge reached up. William held the machine up, fractionally, missed both elms by inches, and saw the wire right ahead of him. Lined up for instant decapitation, he flung the lever forward and instinctively ducked. He half-expected to get hung up by the upper wing, but the Farman plummeted with unexpected alacrity and dropped beneath the wire with what sounded to William like a scream of fright. William saw the ground leap up to meet him. His stiff leg flinched. He hauled on the control stick, fast, still praying, and the ground disappeared abruptly. He felt the tail wheel strike, and grabbed a strut. The undercarriage then hit the ground with an almighty bounce, and the biplane came to a halt in a smother of mud, its skids throwing up great clods of mud and cow-dung.

William let go of the strut and sat still for a minute, pushing up his goggles and easing the cap on his forehead. He felt chastened and a bit weak in the legs.

'But you're still here, boy,' he muttered to himself. He turned round, releasing his waist-strap. 'What's more, so are you, old girl,' he said to the machine.

He knew then that it was all right. He had acquitted himself in difficult circumstances. He was completely undamaged, and so was the machine. So was the farmer's wire.

By the time Sandy and Dorothy arrived in a small motor-car, William was involved in cleaning the distributor with the end of Sandy's scarf, which looked as if it was used quite regularly for such jobs. Sandy walked across the field, eyeing the Farman's position in relation to the electric wire, the hedge and the elm-trees.

'Over the hedge and *under* the wire?' he queried.

'Yes, sir,' William replied, now feeling very uncertain.

But Sandy grinned. 'By jiminy, but that's a new permutation! We've never had that before. We've had *through* the hedge and under the wire, and we've had over the hedge and into the wire, but never over and under. I'd like to have seen you do that.'

'Yes.' William felt rather the same, now. 'I'm sorry, sir, there wasn't anything else I could do.'

'Sorry about what? I wish everyone else got them down in an emergency as neatly as that. That wire will kill somebody one of these days. We've tried to get the old boy to move it, but he won't have it. Have you fixed the engine? What is it? Do you know?'

'Just dirt,' William said.

'If you can get her going again, we'll take her back before it gets dark. You can drive the motor back, can't you?' he said to Dorothy.

'I think so,' Dorothy said.

'This engine's in awful shape,' William said.

'Oh, don't tell me, I know. It needs new piston rings. But we can't leave it out here. If you can just get it to turn over, we should be able to nurse her back to the shed. You can be passenger this time. All right?'

'Yes, if I just tighten this up. Have you got a spanner?'

Sandy seemed quite happy for William to do whatever he wanted with the engine, and fetched some tools from the motor-car. But as it was nearly dark, William only did what was necessary to get the engine to fire again, then, with Sandy at the controls, the Farman took off again. Sandy handled the machine with a familiarity that awed William, flying her nearly at ground level all the way back, skimming between trees and round the odd barn with the occasional bank that brought her wing-tips almost on to the grass. He landed her very accurately, in such a way that she came to a halt right outside her own shed, where the miserable mechanic was waiting with Mr. Adams. Sandy swung round and said to William, 'Don't say anything. I'll get us out of this,' winked at him, and jumped down.

The proprietor stood gnawing the side of his thumb, looking annoyed.

'What's wrong now? She came down, didn't she?'

'Yes, sir. Bill here came out and got her going again.'

'It's nothing much then?' Adams turned to William.

'Well, it's a bit of everything. The whole engine needs overhauling. She won't be reliable until it's done.' William felt a pang for the mechanic, saying this, but knew that he would feel a greater pang for Mr. Pritchard, should he break his neck in the morning.

'I'm not paying a hundred quid to send that motor back to the makers,' Adams said. 'I'm running at a loss as it is.'

'I could do it,' William said.

'How do I know it'll be any better when you've done it? All you lads think you know everything.'

'He got it going quick enough back there,' Sandy put in.

'I wouldn't offer to do it if I didn't know I could,' William said.

Adams, under pressure, hesitated. William, jittery at coming so close to the longed-for opportunity, bit his lip to stop himself from saying any more. Adams, he could judge, was hard and mean, but intelligent enough. Also a liar: William did not see how he could possibly be working at a loss. He was a man who made money out of anything that was currently a money-making project, and teaching people to fly, in 1912, was just that. Or, if he was working at a loss, it was because he did not employ an efficient mechanic.

'I'll take a chance on you then,' Adams said. 'Start whenever you like. I'll put Pritchard off,' he added to Sandy. 'You show Bill anything he wants.' To the mechanic he said, 'You can go back to chauffeuring. You shouldn't ever have left it.'

'No, sir.' The man looked relieved, rather than upset.

The two of them walked away, leaving William standing with Sandy beside the Farman. It was almost dark. William looked at Sandy. Sandy winked again.

'All right?' he said.

'Yes,' William said. 'Oh, yes.'

CHAPTER 3

'Go and answer the door, Christina.'

'Yes, Aunt Grace.'

Christina put down the cotton-box and went out into the draughty hall. Mrs. Astley was coming to be fitted for the dress for her daughter's wedding. A pity, Christina thought, to use such lovely stuff on such an ugly woman. She opened the door.

'*William!*'

She flung herself on him without a thought for decorum, the whole fantastic boredom of the last four weeks dissolving into an explosion of joy. It was no lover's embrace; it was an embrace for all she wished for and loved, and did not have, everything she missed so drastically since exchanging Battersea for Flambards. She buried her face, almost sobbing, into the tweed shoulder.

'Will, oh Will! I'm so glad you've come back!'

William, amazed and blushing furiously, disentangled himself hastily as a cold voice behind him said, 'Mrs. Astley to see Mrs. Marchant, when you've *quite* finished, Christina.'

'Oh, yes,' Christina said, lifting a glowing face. 'Come in. Do come in.'

William stood back for his aunt's customer, who sailed past him with a look that deepened his blushes still further. Christina did not notice. She smiled ecstatically to Aunt Grace who appeared at the door of her sewing-room.

'Look, Will's come back!'

'Good morning, Mrs. Astley. Good morning, William,' said Aunt Grace. 'Go and make us a pot of tea, if you please, Christina. You may go through into the kitchen, William.' Aunt Grace was completely in charge of the situation, as always. But William was glad she had not appeared a moment sooner. He followed Christina through into the small gleaming kitchen, still somewhat astonished by his reception. He had been so fully occupied the last four weeks that, in truth, he had not had much time to think about Christina. He looked at her now with fresh eyes, as if she were a new aircraft. Up till now, living with her as a sister, he had very much taken her for granted. He now saw, quite suddenly, that he could take her for granted no longer.

'Oh, Will, you can't imagine what a relief it is to see you again! I thought I would go mad, until your letter came. It was weeks—I thought you'd been killed! Take your coat off. Here, sit by the fire. Oh, Will—I've been longing for you to come! What have you been doing? Is it all right? You've got a job?'

'I'm sorry—I didn't think—there wasn't anything to tell you, I suppose, so I didn't write.' He had never felt any compulsion to write during the weeks he had lived in the hayloft. 'It wasn't—hasn't been—as easy as I thought, but I think the worst is over now.'

'You've got a job?'

'Of a sort, yes. I'm a mechanic for a flying-school. Only two old crates to look after. It's not much.'

'Oh, but it's something, it means you're in, doesn't it? Not starving.'

'Not quite. No. I'm only getting thirty shillings a week, though. I live in the shed with the machines, so I've only got my food to buy, and the rest I'm trying to save so that I can build my own machine.'

'Couldn't you get a job flying?'

'No, it's not so easy as you think. And—' he hesitated and grimaced down at his stiff leg—'this is the trouble really.'

'But it was no trouble when you flew at home.'

'No. But I can't adapt the school machines just for *my* leg, can I? I *can* fly the Farman, but it's jolly awkward. I can't fly the Blériot at all.'

He paused, and was glad that Christina did not say, 'I told you so,' which she was well entitled to do. Instead she said, very practical like her aunt, 'Perhaps it could be put right. Nobody's ever seen it since Dr. Porter five years ago.'

'Well, that's why I've come up to London,' William said. 'There's a girl at the flying-school, Dorothy Saunders, whose uncle is a doctor in Harley Street. She told me to go and see him. I've got his address here, and two weeks' wages to pay for the visit. If he just told me, I'd know where I was. If it's no good I'll just have to accept it, but if there is anything—well, I could start saving up. He would tell me what it would cost, I should think.'

Christina sat on the edge of the table, frowning into the fire. She took in that William had come up to London, not to see her, but to see a doctor, and that he had met a girl called Dorothy Saunders who was interested in flying, but she tried not to be bothered by such details. She tried to think about the money.

'It would be a lot, I should think.'

'Yes, probably.'

'Perhaps I could get it out of my money on trust.'

'No. I wouldn't take it. I would have to earn it myself, however long it took. I would rather he said it could be done, you see, whatever the effort it would take to save the money, than that he just said it was no good.'

'I could earn some money too,' Christina said. 'I could get a job.'

William looked at her doubtfully.

Christina slipped off the table and held her hands out to the fire. 'I can't stay here,' she said. 'I shall go mad. I can't bear it.'

'Oh.' William could understand that, but did not see any alternative. 'What else can you do?'

'What I'd like to do is get a job near where you are working, so that we can see each other more often. I would do anything, even domestic service. Anything would be better than sewing.'

William considered. He recalled Sandy and Dorothy laughing together in the steamy little café, and thought that it would be very pleasant to have Christina beside him over the cups of tea sometimes. Perhaps she could even learn to fly . . . He smiled.

'What's funny?' she asked.

'I was thinking you could live down there, and be someone's parlour-maid—there are quite a few big houses around—and Sandy could teach you to fly. I bet you'd be the first flying parlour-maid in Britain.'

'Why, does this Dorothy fly then?'

'Yes.'

Christina was silent. She would be as terrified of flying as Will had been of jumping the big grey hunter that had smashed his leg.

'Who's Sandy?'

'Sandy is the instructor. Nice. He goes with Dorothy.'

'Is Dorothy a parlour-maid?'

'No fear. She's rich. Her father owns a hotel.'

'She might know about a job for me. Does she live near the flying-place?'

'Yes, I think she does. I'll ask her if you like. Do you think Aunt Grace would let you go?'

'No, but we'll bother about that when we come to it. Oh, gracious me, she wanted a pot of tea! Shove the kettle on, quickly. I'll set the tray. Oh, Will, I do hate it here! Not Aunt Grace, you understand, who is very kind, but just what we do all day. It's so dull! All those underclothes, and pinning hems, and all those Mrs. Astleys—they're all the same. And making tea, and shopping—' She shrugged and broke off. 'We knew, of course. I mean, I knew, but—oh dear—' She reached for the teapot.

William, seeing her again on her galloping horses, guessed how she felt. They had run away from Flambards with such abandon . . . even he, at times, felt a pang for his comfortable bed, and the great jugfuls of hot water old Mary had brought up in the morning.

'I say, do you think I can have a bath before I go and see this doctor fellow? It's very hard, keeping clean in that old shed.'

Christina looked at him quizzically. 'Why, so it is,' she said, smiling. 'You're quite *grey*.'

He was thinner than ever, she thought, all bones and black eyes.

'I'll go out and get a shave and a haircut and then I'll look as if I can pay his bills. He might not bother if I look too much of a tramp.'

'I'll show you how the geyser works—'

'Christina!' Aunt Grace's voice floated out of the hall.

'Oh, heavens! The tea!'

Christina had to spend the rest of the morning holding pins and handing scissors, listening to William upstairs finding out for himself how the geyser worked, and making up dreams about the future. She was excited, and dreamy and unsettled, her eyes glowing and musing, her mind patently not on her work.

'Really, Christina!' Aunt Grace was exasperated with her, and Mrs. Astley gave her some hard, unkind looks.

'Will's gone to see a doctor about his leg,' she told her aunt when the client had gone.

'How very sensible,' Aunt Grace said. 'Pick up all those cottons, dear, and I'll go and cut a little of that mutton for our lunch.'

Christina tidied up, and ate her lunch, her eyes in Harley Street. It might be just a little thing, after all these years, she thought; a country doctor like Dr. Porter didn't know anything. But when William came back he looked drawn and tired.

'What is it?'

William shook his head. 'He said there's no one in London that could do it. Only—only one surgeon who might—in Switzerland.'

'In Switzerland!'

'Useless, isn't it? I'd rather he'd said there was nobody at all, I think. To save up *that* much money—' William, although having tried to convince himself that it didn't matter, was bitterly disappointed. He said, 'If I want to fly, I've got to build my own controls. That's all right, but it won't get me any work. A working pilot has got to be able to fly anything. I wouldn't mind if I can get a job designing—but the only way I can do that is by building my own machines and proving that they work, which brings me back to money again. I shall never be able to build a machine on a mechanic's wages. It's a tangle.'

'It will sort itself out,' Christina said. 'Even if it's hard now, eventually you will do what you want, leg or no leg.'

'Yes, well, other people have done it. Alliot Roe had no money. He flew one of his first machines with an engine on approval, which he had to send back afterwards. And now look at the Avro D—that's been successful all right. He did it.'

'The way to earn money,' he said, 'is to go in for competitions and win a few prizes. If only I had *Emma*, I could win some money.'

'What sort of competitions?'

'They have them for everything—cross-country, round London, quick-starting, racing round pylons. You can earn money just by giving exhibitions, or taking up passengers—lots of ways, if you have a good machine.'

'Couldn't you borrow her to go in for competitions?'

'I believe Mr. Dermot is rebuilding her again. I got a letter from Joe and he says the old boy's decided to turn her into a monoplane. That's a pretty basic alteration. I should think he'll be starting from scratch again.' William gave a mighty yawn, and looked at the clock. 'I must go back.'

'Not tonight!'

'Yes, I'm on duty at six in the morning. First lesson's at six.'

'Will, please remember what you said about seeing if there are any jobs—'

'Yes, I'll ask Sandy. He knows the neighbourhood pretty well.'

'What's Sandy like?'

'Funny. Easy-going. Works very hard though.'

'And Dorothy?'

'*Very* pretty.' William grinned at Christina. 'Very flirty. Sandy's fallen for her in a big way. He told me he reckons he's the first man to kiss a girl at five hundred feet.'

Christina was shocked. 'She must be very fast!'

'All of sixty miles an hour,' William agreed.

'Don't tease. I didn't know girls flew.'

'No. She's the only one I've come across, apart from those two who've taken their tickets—Mrs. Hewlett and Mrs. What's-her-name—Stocks.' William got to his feet with another yawn. 'I'll find you a job, and you can come and have a look at her. You could fly the wings off her, if you had a chance, Christina. If you were to fly like you ride—'

'It doesn't follow,' Christina said quickly, a sickening twinge of fear hurrying her words. 'If *you* flew like you used to ride—'

'I'd have been dead long ago,' William said easily. 'Perhaps you're right.'

'How do you go from here?' Christina wanted to change the subject.

'I'll walk up to Clapham Junction and take the train. It's quite easy. I go to Kingston, and get a motor bus. If you get a job out there you will be able to visit Aunt Grace quite easily. You must tell her that. She probably won't like the idea. . . .'

William was right. Aunt Grace didn't.

'Gadding about with a lot of young men and no chaperone! It would be most unseemly, Christina.'

'But I should be working. There wouldn't be any time for gadding about.'

'Working at what, I should like to know?'

So would Christina, but she bit back her words. She thought Aunt Grace would get used to the idea, slowly. She had done some gadding about herself, in her own time, but Christina knew that elderly people did not like such arguments used against them.

'I won't have you living in diggings, whatever happens.' Aunt Grace was adamant. 'A place in a superior household, possibly— although how you could possibly prefer domestic service to staying comfortably here I do not know. You're too well-bred for such a thing.'

'I would like to be independent, Aunt Grace.'

'That's the trouble with you young people today. You're *too* independent. When I was a girl we did what we were told. . . . '

All old people were the same, Christina thought. She longed to meet Sandy, and Dorothy, and go for walks with Will after work. She sat unpicking a long seam that had been put in wrong, dreaming of being independent.

'A post as governess would be more suitable,' Aunt Grace was saying. 'Although you are such a dreamer, I'm sure I don't know that the poor pupils would learn anything. You are unpicking the wrong seam, Christina!'

When Will's letter came at last, addressed in his small, rapid writing, Christina tore it open with a sense of desperation. As if sensing her feelings, William had come straight to the point:

'Dear Christina,

'I have inquired about a job for you, and Dorothy says that if you go and see her father he will probably find you a position. He has several hotels, including one at Kingston, and she thinks he would very likely fix you something there. This would be very handy for Elm Park. She suggests you come over to Kingston on Tuesday, when her father will be there. . . .'

Christina tilted the letter in Aunt Grace's curious direction, having seen that there was nothing that would offend her. Dorothy Saunders seemed to be very usefully connected, with her hotel-owning father and Harley Street uncle. Christina was deeply suspicious of this well-favoured girl, who could fly an aeroplane and kiss a man at the same time.

'An hotel!' Aunt Grace was saying. 'Surely you would not consider anything so low, Christina! I'm surprised that William should even suggest such a thing.'

'It might be a very high-class hotel, Aunt Grace. I should not think Will would recommend anything unsuitable.'

'That young man has no more idea of what is suitable and what is not than you have.'

'But you will allow me to meet Mr. Saunders?'

'We shall both meet him,' Aunt Grace said firmly.

It was the best Christina could manage. She would have far rather gone by herself, but better to go with Aunt Grace than not at all.

The housekeeper at Flambards had sent her clothes in a travelling-trunk, and Christina went to choose something suitable to wear for her interview. Taking up most of the room in the trunk was her black riding habit, made for her by the best tailor in Essex (her riding clothes were the only clothes Uncle Russell had bought for her in five years. The others had been sent by Aunt Grace). The beautifully cut jacket prompted a small sigh. There were still spots of Essex mud here and there, and a smear of horse-sweat . . . Woodpigeon, or Drummer, Christina thought, with a pang. It was the end of May. The horses would have been turned out for the summer now and the chestnuts would have flowered. The awful homesickness rose up in Christina again, strong and unquenchable and unbidden, so that she shook with it, clenching her hands over the trunk. She could smell the horses, and hear

Mark shouting at the old foxhounds, and see the sun flooding the tangled covert. 'Oh, God,' she thought. 'Take it away! Please make Kingston be all right. Please make it work! Please let everything come right!'

On the morning of the interview she looked neat and industrious in a lilac-grey tunic coat and a wide-brimmed but unexotic hat. She pinned her hair back tidily and borrowed a pair of gloves from Aunt Grace. Aunt Grace was disapproving in black. Christina was very nervous, and very excited. So much depended on this interview, and she was terrified of being a failure, and being immured in Battersea for the summer. The pavements were hot beneath the sun, the soot flecked her face as the steam trains roared over the iron bridge. It was wonderful to be outside, and heading away from the tangled traffic and shoving pedestrians. Christina went on praying. She hated Battersea. She hated the rumble of iron-hooped wheels over the setts and the white faces of the factory girls. Kingston will be quiet and pretty, she thought, with rowing-boats on the river, and pony carts going out into the country down the Portsmouth Road.

Kingston was not as she imagined, but she liked it. It had an air of prosperous suburbia mixed with the quaintness of a country market town. It was more sophisticated than the Essex towns she had visited, with as many motors as horses; it had a music-hall and a picture-palace, but shady trees by the river and men fishing. She tried not to commit herself, to be prepared for going back to Battersea and facing a summer of sewing, but she knew she would not be able to do it. 'Even if it's emptying chamber-pots, I will stay here,' she thought. 'Aunt Grace will not stop me.' A few miles up the road Will was working over his oily engines; in the evenings they would meet, and walk by the river. Or hire a skiff with velvet cushions. Christina's hands were sticky in the black kid gloves.

'This is it then,' Aunt Grace decided.

'The Bunch of Grapes' looked perfectly respectable, to Christina's infinite relief. It lay just off the market-place, fronting the main road, and appeared to cater for business men and travellers. Aunt Grace read the menu that was pinned beside the front door and said, 'It's not cheap, I'll give it that.' Christina sensed approval in her tone, and started to prickle with nerves. Aunt Grace swept regally through the doors and up to the reception desk, Christina meekly following.

'Miss Parsons and Mrs. Marchant to see Mr. Saunders, if you please,' she announced to the elderly receptionist.

'Just a moment, please, madam.' The receptionist disappeared and returned with an auburn-haired girl. Christina and Dorothy looked at each other coolly, instinctively on guard. Christina saw instantly what Will had meant by 'flirty'; she herself would have called it by a stronger word. The girl was exceedingly attractive, and aware of it, not playing down her charms in any way at all. She had a strong, sensual face, with perfect features, and a very smart, dark-green dress (Christina noticed Aunt Grace capturing it professionally with a hawk-like glance) which set off her colouring to its best advantage. Her very evident poise, as well as her striking appearance, made Christina feel gauche by comparison, aware of her wishy-washy dress and dull hat. She felt at an immediate disadvantage, and resented it with all the nervous sensibility of her seventeen years.

'My father will see you as soon as he has finished with the brewer,' she said. 'Will you come through?'

She lifted a flap in the reception counter, and ushered them through into an office at the back.

'You're Christina?' she said, smiling. 'Bill has told me about you.'

'Oh? Will has told me about you too,' she replied coolly. If she had added, 'Kissing at five hundred feet,' she knew that Dorothy would not have been at all put out. She would have laughed. Christina remembered that she wanted the job very badly, and smiled.

Dorothy said, 'He's made a wonderful difference at the airfield. Both machines are quite reliable since he's worked on them. They never were before, you know—always conking out, or falling to bits. It's made life much easier for Sandy.'

'Yes, of course.' Christina's hostility melted a little. How could this girl fly? she wondered. How could she sit there, up in the sky, knowing that the machine was liable—how did she put it—to conk out, or fall to bits? Her boldness was not mere sex appeal. It was a physical courage before which Christina felt chastened. If she had felt that Will was serious about her learning to fly, she thought she would have gone back to Flambards.

Before they could make any more conversation, Mr. Saunders came in, and Aunt Grace took over on Christina's behalf. Christina wondered who was interviewing whom, but held her tongue miserably. Mr. Saunders was auburn like his daughter, but quiet and firm-lipped. While Aunt Grace talked he looked closely at Christina, up and down, and Christina held herself stiffly, praying under her breath.

'Can you use a typewriting machine?' he said to her suddenly.

'No, sir. But I could learn.'

'You can add up?'

'Yes, sir.'

'Show me your writing.' He pushed a pad of paper and a pen at her over the desk, and she wrote her name and Battersea address very quickly and neatly, to his evident approval.

'You look sharp enough,' he commented. 'The receptionist here is retiring next year. If you learn to use a typewriting machine, and work the switchboard, you can train to take over her job. It's a bit of everything, you understand. Tact and common sense in large quantities required. You can fill in with being a waitress for the first few months. A room in the attic, all your meals, two half-days off a week, and half a crown a week to start with—all right?'

Christina's mouth fell open in surprise. She shut it hastily and said, 'Yes! Oh, yes, sir!'

She looked at Aunt Grace, who was obviously trying to work out any snags. 'She's never lived away from home before, you understand, Mr. Saunders? She's very young. If you can assure me——'

'Madam, I understand your anxiety. Mrs. Carter, our house-keeper, looks after all the girls like a mother. You may meet her if you wish, and she will show you where the girls sleep. Miss Parsons will have a room of her own, of course. I'm sure you will be very satisfied with the arrangements.'

'In that case——' Aunt Grace said dourly.

Christina's heart was singing. She wanted to leap off her seat and embrace the little man. When Dorothy reappeared she beamed at her. Mr. Saunders was called away to the telephone and Christina said, 'Thank you very much for asking your father to see me. It was very kind of you.'

'Anything for a friend,' Dorothy said casually. And Christina wondered suddenly if she was the friend, or 'Bill'.

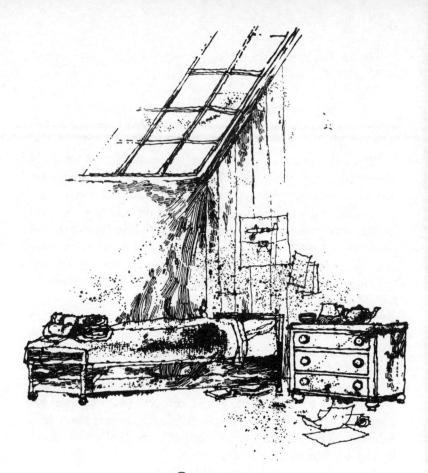

Chapter 4

The wooden hangar had a glass sheet in the roof at the far end,
and the sun streamed through it, illuminating a truckle bed with
some blankets folded neatly on it, a very dilapidated chest of
drawers and a work bench strewn with papers and drawings. A
naked electric light bulb hung over the work-bench, and an oil-
drum served for a chair.

'You mean this is where you live?'

Christina looked at the scene blankly. To her it resembled a
sepia drawing she had once seen illustrating the garret in the opera
'La Bohème'. Only this was real.

'It's all I need,' William said, somewhat apologetically. 'It's a bit of a squash when both the machines are in, mind you.'

'But—but where do you sit?'

'I don't entertain, if that's what you mean,' Will said, grinning at her. 'I work on the drawings nearly every evening, which means that I sit on the oil-drum. Then I go to bed. What more do I want?'

Christina had thought that her own room at 'The Bunch of Grapes' was slightly spartan, but by comparison with William's hangar it was a palace.

'I'm not the only living-in mechanic down here,' William was saying. 'I'm not short of company, if I fancy it. Look.' He walked with her to the door of the shed. There were over thirty sheds in the row, twenty-five of which were rented for housing machines.

'Besides the three flying-schools, there are six sheds where people are building their own machines, ten with private—mostly French—machines in, and six with various old crates that give flips. So you can see there's plenty of congenial company. Bit different from Mr. Dermot's place, eh?'

Christina looked doubtfully at William. He wore a pair of black overalls, shining with grease, and an oily black cap. His hands were engrained with black oil, and his forehead smeared where he had pushed back his matching black hair. He looked completely happy.

'If you could get a Saturday or a Sunday off and come down here,' he said, 'you'd really see some flying. Everyone's out then. Some week-ends they have competitions here—you'd be surprised at the number of spectators that turn up. That's when the joy-ride people make their money.'

'Do you ever get a chance to fly?'

'No. Only across the field sometimes, if somebody leaves them in the wrong place.'

The field was large and flat. On the far side a pair of horses were pulling a reaper, making hay, the driver keeping an anxious eye on the old Farman that blipped overhead. Beyond the field was undulating heath and farmland with 'too many trees for comfort', according to Sandy. The sheds lay in a long line all down one side. Behind them were offices and garages, and outside the main road which brought the spectators and the enthusiasts out from London. In the warm June sunshine it seemed to Christina that the intense enthusiasm she had first sensed in Mr. Dermot's old shed at home, when Will had worked over *Emma* with Joe and Jack, Mr. Dermot's mechanics, emanated from these Elm Park sheds in just the same way. Even from a distance of over a hundred yards she could sense the drama of a little group whose machine had broken its undercarriage in a too impetuous landing —'They'll have to work all night on that,' William remarked, 'because he's flying it at Hendon tomorrow'—and nearer at hand there was no mistaking the passion in the voice of the young man who jumped out of his motor and met his mechanic with, 'You've fixed that pressure pump, have you? She's fit now?' 'Yes, sir, ready to go.'

William said to Christina, 'He divides his time between big-game hunting in Africa and flying, that chap. I think his life's ambition is to combine the two. Fly to Africa——.'

Christina laughed. 'Gracious, he's optimistic!'

But William said solemnly, 'Oh, no, I don't think so.'

The Farman was approaching the runway from over the trees at the far end and they turned to watch it.

'Looks as if Dorothy's at the controls,' William said, as the wings wobbled erratically. 'I bet Sandy's sweating!' He seemed amused, but Christina felt a pulse of anxiety beating in her throat.

'Is she all right?'

'She's a bit high.'

'She won't crash, will she?' Christina's face was screwed up, her body braced with fear.

William looked at her and laughed. 'Not if Sandy's got anything to do with it! You watch.'

The Farman lurched towards them, its engine cut out. Christina could see the muffled figure of Dorothy, leaning forward, trying to judge her height above the racing grass, her left arm clutching the strut in anticipation of the shock. Behind her, Sandy reached forward suddenly, closing his hand over hers on the lever. The nose of the machine dropped with a swoop, then reared up, and the machine bounced with a shrieking and straining of its parts that made William wince.

'That will be another set of shock absorbers for me to fix!'

Christina had shut her eyes at the last moment, and opened them in time to see the Farman bounce to a standstill with its nose only thirty feet from the perimeter railings.

'Better new shock absorbers for the Farman than a new wall for the café,' William remarked, and they walked over to where Sandy and Dorothy were jumping down.

'She'll kill me yet!' Sandy shouted cheerfully. Dorothy, to Christina's surprise, was laughing.

'I keep trying,' she said. She pulled off layers of scarves and shook out the dishevelled mass of her auburn hair. 'I thought that was going to be a good one, till the last moment.'

'It would have been a good one if the airfield was a mile longer,' Sandy said.

William laughed. He turned to Christina and said, 'Why don't you try sitting up there, just see what it's like?'

'Yes, come on,' Sandy said immediately. 'You can roll it across the field. Young Matthews hasn't arrived yet, has he?' He glanced over towards the shed. 'I can't see his jalopy. Come on, free flips for females. Old Adams has gone to Brooklands so there's no one to see.'

He took Christina's elbow and walked her forward so that she stood right below the pilot's frail seat. She recoiled instinctively, glancing up at the sunlit panoplies of stretched fabric and glinting wires.

'Oh, no!'

'Here, take my coat and scarf,' Dorothy said. 'You'll love it if you just try it. You must find out what it's all about, surely?'

'Of course she must,' Will said. 'Come on, Christina, put them on.'

Christina, pressed by the three of them, put on the coat and wound the scarf round her head in silence. She was so frightened that she was afraid she was going to pass out. She tried to take a long steady breath to calm herself; it was impossible to speak. Yet Dorothy and the two boys were so easy about the incident that they did not notice her concern. Even in that moment of real, deep fear, she knew she must keep her head and pass it off, and never be so humiliated as to show her feelings. She said nothing, but forced herself to get up into the seat. Sandy got up with her and started telling her what to do, and Will and Dorothy chatted and laughed down on the grass. Christina braced herself rigid, petrified that Sandy would notice her trembling.

'Just the length of the field and back. I'll turn her, then you can see if you can make her hop. You'll have to work the rudder. I can't reach it from here. When I say "Left foot" or "Right foot" push fairly hard. It needs a lot of pressure on the ground. Not upstairs though. Got it? All right, Will. We're ready. Switch on, Christina. That knob down on your left. If we look as if we're going to hit the fence before we get round, switch off again. Will'll help her round. Right foot, Christina. Hard.'

Sandy bawled in her ear above the sudden burst of the engine, and Christina felt the machine lurch beneath her. She lunged out with her foot, frantically, and moaned into Dorothy's muffler. The fight for her self-control was as desperate as her struggle with the machine. 'I must—I *must*——' her mind was crying out, and it was as much to find courage, as to know what to do with her feet. She saw the fence railings moving round the left wing-tip, and Will's face momentarily. The grass started to move beneath her, and the racket in her ears was deafening.

'Rudder straight, Christina!' Sandy bawled. 'Left foot, straighten up! That's it, as she is!'

Tears streamed from her eyes. The grass started to run, faster and faster. 'Will!' she cried out. 'Oh, no!' She felt the wind thrusting at her and the grotesque machine plunging and straining, the ground bounding . . . The panic rose up. 'Sandy!' she screamed.

Sandy's hand closed over hers, warm and huge. His own fingers pushed her hand an inch forward on the lever, then drew it back, very calm and very easy. His head was right beside hers, she felt the rough tweed of his cap on her cheek. He shouted something and the Farman was suddenly smooth, all the jarring and shuddering dropped away. She felt a nauseating swing in the pit of her stomach, as if all her guts had come loose, and an utter bewilder-ment in her mind, her brains blown to the four winds.

Sandy shouted something again. 'Switch off!' He jabbed his finger towards the petrol switch, and she grabbed it, fumbling. There was a silence as shattering as the roar that preceded it, and Sandy's warm hand pushed on hers again. The next moment the Farman had touched down with the mildest of bounces, and was rolling to a standstill. The journey had taken mere seconds. Chris-tina felt that she had just come to from a nightmare; her body was shaking all over.

She let go of the lever and buried her face in her hands. She felt Sandy's arm round her, and was aware of a skylark singing somewhere above her head.

'Come, come, tootsie.' Sandy's voice was gentle. 'It's not as bad as all that, is it?'

Christina opened her eyes and saw Sandy's face close beside hers, his grey eyes very kind, not mocking at all. She shook her head, not daring to trust her voice.

'There's nothing to it, not in this old grasshopper,' he said. 'Don't be afraid. I won't let anything go wrong.'

Strangely, his gentleness reminded her of Dick, the groom at Flambards, who had comforted her in her early riding days. Humiliated by her fear, she knew, quite surely, that flying would never come to her as riding had. If she was fated to fly, the most she could hope for was to learn to hide her feelings. So far, she had not done very well.

'I'm all right,' she said, in a voice very strange to her own ears.

'Come on, then, switch on. We'll roll back. No hurry.'

It seemed that the machine could be made to trundle along the ground by switching the engine on until she gathered speed, then switching it off to slow her down, then on again. After the shock of leaving the ground altogether, this was not quite so alarming. Sandy shouted at her when to operate the switch, and kept one hand on her shoulder. Surging and bouncing, the old Farman made her way across the field, past the machine with the buckled undercarriage, and the snorting horses cutting hay. In the last silence before it rolled to a standstill by the sheds, Christina turned her head and said to Sandy, 'Don't . . . don't tell Will how frightened I was.'

'No,' said Sandy. 'You were fine.'

But Christina knew she had not hidden it from Sandy. She also knew that, if it had been Will with her, flying the Farman, he would have laughed at her. He would not have been gentle like Sandy. She was infinitely grateful for Sandy's tact.

Sandy's next pupil, a eager young man of about twenty with a striped blazer and a boater, was waiting outside the shed. Will was occupied with getting him the school flying-clothes, and Christina was relieved that she could jump down and gather her wits together before meeting his eyes. Dorothy was waiting, laughing.

'You did a much better landing than I did!' she called out, confident of her own superiority. 'Fun, wasn't it?'

'Oh—yes!' Christina felt herself going crimson, unwinding the scarf from her hair. She looked up at Sandy, and was comforted by a wink.

'Let's go for a cup of tea,' Dorothy said. 'Are you coming, Bill?'

'In a minute,' Will said. 'When we've got the bus off again. Don't wait for me.'

'They go on all day,' Dorothy grumbled to Christina as they walked away across the grass together. 'I don't know how they stand it. Sandy does fourteen hours sometimes, now the days are so long. And Bill has to work all night if something gets broken. They're all crazy, these aeronauts.'

'They like it though,' Christina said. She was thinking of sewing for Aunt Grace.

'Do you like it, in the hotel?' Dorothy asked suddenly.

'Oh—yes. It seemed very strange at first, but now—yes, I think I shall like it.' The first week at 'The Bunch of Grapes' had rolled over Christina like a hurricane over a blown leaf. Now on her first free afternoon, she felt that she had survived the initial onslaught; that she would make her own way, with luck. 'I like it much better than living with my aunt,' she added.

'Oh, heavens, I should think so.'

The café had some outdoor tables, laid in the sunshine, where the two girls sat down. There was a smell of trodden grass and dust, and the buzzing of the Farman drove off the remnants of Christina's shock. She leaned back in her chair, turning her face to the sun, happy, grateful for the comfort of terra firma which had so recently been denied her. The smell of the hay and the distant whirring of the reaper was the sweetest cure she could have wished for.

The waitress came to the table with a letter. 'If Mr. Russell is going to join you, Miss Saunders, this letter came for him yesterday.'

'Thank you. He'll be here in a minute.'

Christina looked at the envelope lying on the table. The postmark was their home village in Essex, but the writing was not Will's father's, nor Mark's, nor even old Mary's. It was ill-educated writing, clear and boyish. Christina was curious. When Will came over, looking rather more respectable without his overalls and cap, he picked it up in surprise.

'Whoever's writing to me?'

'I don't know that writing. It's nobody at home,' Christina said.

William tore the envelope open and read the letter, still standing up. Christina saw his expression change. His face went tight with pain, and his eyes filled with tears.

'What is it?' Christina started up from her seat.

'It's Mr. Dermot,' Will said. 'He's killed himself, flying *Emma*. The letter's from Joe.'

'Oh, no!'

William's face seemed to crumple up. 'I—I—can't——' He turned away, scrumpling the letter in his hand. Some mechanics were coming across the grass, laughing and talking. William walked past them, taking no notice of their greetings. He rubbed a hand across his face, and started to run back towards the shed.

CHAPTER 5

William borrowed a black suit from Sandy for the funeral, and drove to Essex in Sandy's model T Ford. It was a very hot day, almost midsummer, too bumpy for easy flying. While William drove along the dusty country roads, Christina in her sober grey uniform propped open the doors of the hotel with pots of geraniums to make a through draught, and tried to keep her sticky fingers from making smears in the ledgers. There were a lot of thirsty customers at the bar, and the cook sent her out to the market for another dozen lettuces, as nobody fancied the roasts. 'Poor Will,' she kept thinking all day, bottled up with his grief and his black suit. Will had loved the eccentric Mr. Dermot, and had been adamant about attending the funeral.

'Just for a friend?' Mr. Adams had queried suspiciously. 'It's not a relation?'

'No. He's *more* than my father. For my father I would stay here and work on your blasted machines all day, but for Mr. Dermot I am going.'

Sandy had thought William would lose his job altogether, overhearing the exchange in the office, but Mr. Adams, either putting the outburst down to the pressure of grief, or possibly knowing when he had found a good mechanic, agreed without another word.

'Just the one day. We can't do without you on Saturday morning.'

Christina finished work at seven, and rode out on Mrs. Carter's bicycle to Elm Park to see if William had returned. She enjoyed her bicycle rides, and revelled in the odd hours of freedom she snatched, pedalling along the roads over the wide Surrey commons where the gorse was ablaze and the rabbits flicked their white scuts. The smell of June, the beginning of the freshness of evening, of trampled earth and blown dust, the suggestion of cooking from an open doorway, made her want to sing, and she ached for Mr. Dermot, not that he was dead, but that he was dead in June, when his flying sky was soft and cloudless like blue silk and his landing strip starred and thick with buttercups. 'January is for dying,' she thought. And she loved Will as she rode along, because he had cried for Mr. Dermot, and he was overworked, and she wanted to meet him and comfort him.

Sandy was just finishing when she got there. It was getting cool, and the last of the young men were driving away in their motley cars.

'Why, Christina!' Sandy was surprised, coming up the path to the café.

'I wondered if Will was back.'

'It's a long drive. I should think he'd be pretty late. Come and have something to eat with me.'

Christina thought with a pang of Aunt Grace, and wondered what her opinion would be if she knew that her niece was out on a bicycle, dining *alone* with a young man. Yet the girls in Kingston rode alone on their bicycles, and the women in London were chaining themselves to the railings for the sake of even more privileges. Will had told her that Sandy's mother was a suffragette. Christina watched him over his large plate of steak and kidney pie. He was nineteen, less ambitious than William, quiet, and always kind. She felt very easy with him, almost easier than with Will at times, because nothing between the two of them mattered quite so much—there were no undercurrents of disturbing feelings as there were between herself and Will. And she knew that Sandy, if he was disturbed by anybody, was disturbed by Dorothy, not herself.

'Is it true that your mother is a suffragette?' she asked him.

He nodded. 'Yes, she's inside at the moment. Six months for trying to set the House of Commons on fire.'

Christina was amazed. She tried to think of Aunt Grace behaving in such a manner, and failed.

'She's always been at it, ever since I can remember,' Sandy said. 'That's why I left home. It got pretty gloomy with my father

47

carrying on about it, and cold meat and salad all the time because she was out at meetings, and then the police calling. I packed up.'

Christina was puzzled by it. She did not want to vote, but she wanted to ride a bicycle alone over the common in the evening, and perhaps that was a little of what it meant. If it meant that girls shouldn't stay sewing with their Aunt Graces, but should go out and earn their living, she was all in favour.

'She must be very brave,' she said. She thought she must be a bit like Sandy, not so much brave as thoughtful and patient and dogged and knowing what she wanted. Christina did not envy Sandy his job, any more than she envied Mrs. Hardcastle in prison.

'A bit daft,' Sandy said, grinning. He washed his meal down with half a pint of beer and yawned, comfortably. 'That's better.' He glanced at his watch. 'Poor Bill. The Blériot's got to have new warp wires tonight, if Pritchard's going to take her to Hendon in the morning. I wonder if he remembered? It looks as if he's going to be late.'

'I suppose I ought to get back,' Christina said. 'I've got to be in by dark.' She pushed her chair back.

Sandy lifted his head suddenly, curious. 'What's that? I thought we were all home.'

The sound of an aircraft engine came distinctly on the evening breeze. Sandy, unable to resist the summons, stood up and stared over the field. The engine cut out, but the machine was visible, flashing suddenly over the distant trees as the last of the sun caught some metal work on the fuselage. It was a small monoplane, apparently intending to land, but travelling at a fantastic speed. Sandy pushed his chair back with an urgent scrape.

'The crash corps has gone home to its supper,' he said. 'It looks as if we're going to need it.'

He started to walk quickly over the beaten grass towards the field. Christina hurried after him, gabbling with fear.

'Sandy—it's—oh, Sandy, I'm sure—' The lines of the little machine were so familiar to her that it was almost like being homesick again. It might be a monoplane now, but there was no mistaking the hand of its designer, the jaunty, dragonfly lines. 'It's Will!' she said. 'That's Mr. Dermot's machine!'

48

Sandy turned and grasped her hand. 'Will? It's the bus that killed the old man?' He started to run, with Christina stumbling after him. 'God almighty, I can see why.'

The monoplane hurtled over the grass. The sun, lipping the edges of the peaceful birches, flooded the runway with the last of its light and little *Emma* turned to flying gold and silver, so that for a moment Christina thought she was on fire. The grass flattened, white, in her slipstream; she touched and bounced, and Christina heard the screams of straining wires and timber. High into the air, flimsy and glittering, she leapt, her shadow convulsing itself below. Christina ran, panic catching her, not wanting to look, but unable to turn away. She saw *Emma* plunge again, like a shot bird, bounce in a cloud of sparkling dust so that she almost disappeared from sight, then speed on as if she never intended to come to rest.

'The railings will stop him,' Sandy said. He turned round and Christina saw that he was no longer frightened. 'What an undercarriage!' he said. 'Come on, he'll be all right.'

'Why—why does he have to land like that?' Christina panted, angry with being so frightened.

'It's the machine—he's doing his best!'

They were running over the field, their shadows almost touching the far perimeter. Ahead of them the monoplane wheeled suddenly, digging in one wing. There was a tearing and a crashing and one white wing cartwheeled against the dusk like a flag of surrender.

'That's stopped her!' Sandy shouted. *Emma* scrumpled, mute and vanquished, and Christina smelt the warm dust and the hot, familiar oil reek. It was over. She ran on, trying to take a hold of her feelings, not to show that it mattered. 'But I'm only a human being,' she thought.

William was climbing out, which was not very difficult, as the monoplane lay on its fuselage, one wing buckled beneath it, its nose pointing to the sky. The wire fence of the perimeter was only twenty feet away.

'As long as the engine's all right,' he was saying, 'the rest doesn't matter. I didn't want her to hit the fence. That's seven hundred pounds' worth of motor—it was all I was thinking about.

Joe told me that she took about two miles to land in, but I didn't believe him. I do now.'

'This is what killed the old man?'

'Yes, he only flew her once, and was thrown out when she hit

the ground. She's an absolute crank machine—I don't know what could have possessed him to work out something like this.'

William, having examined his engine, stood back, staring at the wrecked machine. He had a pair of overalls on over Sandy's black suit, and was covered with oil. He pushed his cap up off his greasy forehead, still looking at the machine.

'She's mine,' he said. 'He said I was to have her.'

Christina, standing behind him, thought, 'I should be pleased that he has got what he wanted.' But she didn't feel pleased at all. Will had been safe as a mechanic, but now Christina knew that he was back to normal, with *Emma* to risk his life on whenever he pleased. She might have guessed that the respite would be very short. He looked dazed, as if he had not really had time to take in his tumbling mixture of good and bad fortune.

'She'll need a lot of modifying. You can't leave her to herself for a moment. She'll start to side-slip if you so much as clear your throat. And her wing-loading is suicidal.'

'Come on,' Sandy said. 'Don't start modifying her now. Christina and I thought you were all set for a ride in a coffin a few moments ago. What about my motor-car, anyway?'

William turned round and seemed to see Christina for the first time.

'I'm sorry if I scared you,' he said, with his old grin. He held out his hand to her. 'It's all right, eh? You're pleased, Christina?' He pulled her towards him and she could sense the deep, weary, oily excitement in the hug of his filthy arm. His face was splattered black and lined with exhaustion and he staggered on his stiff leg so that she had to support him, yet there was this shining content that rubbed out all his physical weakness. She could see that he was more happy than she had ever known him. The infection of his bliss made her laugh. It was impossible to resist.

'Oh, of course—'

He hugged her again. 'Christina, I could—oh, lord! I'm sorry. Look what I've done to your blouse!' He let her go, and laughed. 'I'll buy you another one! Oh, Christina, I could—come here—it's wonderful!' He put both arms round her and hugged her, and she felt the oil and grime and sweat sticky on her cheek, and laughed. She buried her nose in his neck. 'Will, it's wonderful! Yes—'

'As I was saying,' Sandy remarked, 'about my motor—'

They laughed. It was as if *Emma*'s crash had sparked off a great fountain of ridiculous joy. They walked back across the field, laughing at the people that came out to meet them. Christina wanted to laugh and cry at the same time, holding on to Will's greasy hand. She thought she had never felt so happy, nor so near to tears, and yet she did not really know why. She had forgotten that it was dark, and that she should go back to the hotel. They sat at a table in the dusk and Will and Sandy talked, and Will ate while he talked, and Christina listened to the blackbird singing in the trees behind the café.

'The warp wires on the Blériot,' Sandy said, when William had finished. 'They'll have to be ready by six. And the skid needs looking at—have you remembered?'

William groaned, 'Oh, no!' He was slumped back in his chair, his eyes half shut. 'Yes, all right. I'll do them.'

'Perhaps I could help you?' Christina said. She did not want to go back to the hotel, not until she had to. The blackbird was still singing, and she felt—she could not have described how she felt.

'What about your Mrs. Carter woman?' William said. 'Counting her maids in the attic? You'll get the sack.'

'I'm going into Kingston to see Dorothy. I'll tell her,' Sandy was saying, as if there was no problem at all. 'I'll tell her you'll be late.' He got up, and remembered. 'Will, you rotter! My motor-car's still in Essex.'

'No, it's on its way. Joe's driving it over. It'll be here soon.'

'I can't wait all night. I'll borrow young Potter's. He won't mind.'

He was gone, and Christina wondered, with a pang, whether she shouldn't have gone with him. She sat tightly, her heart racing, until the motor door slammed and the rackety engine pounded away down the road. Then she knew it was all right, and too late. Will got up, took her hand, and they walked slowly back to the Silver Cloud shed. There were crickets in the grass, and a new moon thin over the perimeter trees where *Emma* had glided so perilously. Will opened the door of the shed and they squeezed in. It was like an oven; Christina felt the sweat prickling on her body, beading her lip.

'Oh, I could sleep!' William stretched out his arms, stifling a great yawn. The shed seemed filled with the spidery, crouching frames of the somnolent machines. The heavy atmosphere was thick with the sickly smell of castor oil and the tang of doped fabric. To Christina it was the strangest stable in the world, yet she knew that to Will it was home. She looked up at him, dubious now, but his content had not left him.

'We'll really get started now, Christina,' he said. 'I've got an engine, that's the marvellous thing. And I can make her into something, poor little *Emma*, to fly until my own machine is ready.'

His voice echoed in the rafters of the shed. He walked down to the bottom, twanging the wires of the Farman as he squeezed round her wing-tips, and switched on the electric light. Christina followed him, blinking at the sudden glare.

'Talk to me, Christina, so that I don't fall asleep, and we'll get this job done. You meant it, when you said you'd help?'

'Yes.'

'You're wonderful, Christina. To do this, and back there, when I smashed *Emma* up, not to fuss and scream—just stand there all calm and not saying anything. I used to worry at first, dragging you into all this. It's not girls' stuff, I suppose—I thought it would all turn out to be a mistake, but now I don't think so.' He was pulling out his tool-box as he spoke, and laying out the things he was going to use. Christina watched his delicate, dirty hands putting everything in order, remembering how she had fought against her panic, and how her insides had felt sick and the sweat had run down her forehead. William was perpetually amazing her: would he ever stop, she wondered. Did he really see her as calm and detached?

'Pass me that spanner on the bench, will you?'

She passed it.

'Girls like Dorothy,' he said, 'are only after a man. She's not really bothered with learning to fly. She's the sort that would catch a man like Sandy, and then spend all her time talking him into taking a smart job with her father or something. There aren't many who see how much it means, as you do.'

Christina flashed a glance at William, but he was involved in detaching the warp wire from beneath the Blériot's wing. She said in a low voice, 'When I've caught you I'm going to spend all my time talking you into taking a safe job with horses.'

William roared with laughter. 'There's no such thing! You know it. *Emma*'s never broken a bone of me yet, but that grey brute—'

'The sweetest horse in Essex,' Christina said.

'God save me from the others! Chris, you—oh, I wish I was a bit cleaner, I'd kiss you again. Look, hold these pliers. Pass me that big screwdriver—no, the one with the red handle—'

Christina laughed. She stood passing tools, holding things,

doing as she was told, and William worked, lapsing into silence as the job became more involved. Christina forgot how he had surprised her. She stood looking down on the back of his head, at the stubble of close-cropped hair behind his ear, at the fingers working quickly and meticulously amongst the disengaged wires, and prayed to God that this feeling of hers would come again after this night was over, that it would come often, because she had never felt so happy before. However the Aunt Graces might sourly castigate, she knew that she was doing no wrong in staying with Will. Nothing could be wrong when she felt like this. Rules and regulations were meaningless.

They opened the hangar doors to let in more air, and beyond the glaring electric light the midsummer sky was a blurr of glowing blue. The moths and the mosquitoes whirred and blundered around their faces. Will worked more slowly, rubbing his eyes wearily. The wire-splicing was tedious and impossible to hurry, and the damage to the skid more severe than it appeared at first sight. It was three o'clock when he finished, and the deep blue sky was softening in the east. He started to pack up his tools, and Christina went to the doors to get some fresh air. The smell of the dew-drenched grass was almost a shock. She stumbled with weariness, and leaned her head against the outside wall, looking across the field. Behind the sheds the birds in the birch woods were starting up their dawn gabble, reminding her piercingly of Essex dawns and cubbing mornings; she almost forgot for a moment where she was, and what she was doing there. Then she saw the lone wing of the crumpled *Emma* across the field, and remembered that she was cool and calm. She smiled, shook her head once more in amazement, and went back into the shed. Will, having sat for a moment on his truckle bed to regard the good work he had accomplished on the Blériot, had been defeated by exhaustion at last, and lay sprawled, still in his working cap and clothes, fast asleep. A mosquito drew blood from his cheek, but he did not stir. Christina switched off the light, and pulled one of the thin blankets over Will, and pushed his cap off. He muttered, but did not move. The shed was getting cool at last, and the light was creeping in over the concrete floor.

Christina walked back across the field to where she had left her bicycle by the gate. She was in a daze of weariness herself; physically she almost reeled as she walked. But mentally it was as if her brain had never seen anything so clearly. As she rode back over the singing, dew-sharp commons she felt that she had discovered during the last few hours what it really meant to be in love with somebody. Before it had been like playing at it, or pretending to herself, all pits of doubt and stabs of adoration in bewildering confusion, as if she was doing something she had read about in books. But tonight it had been real, it had filled her utterly. 'Even if he loves his old machines better than me,' she thought, 'no one else will ever love him as I do.'

And she rode back into Kingston, swaying with exhaustion, on Mrs. Carter's bicycle.

CHAPTER 6

In her rustic ignorance Christina had never supposed that there would be anything but a slight reprimand for her night's absence. She did not expect to be summoned to Mr. Saunders' office at nine o'clock in the morning, and be confronted there by the wrath of Mrs. Carter.

'Mrs. Carter tells me you have been out all night, Miss Parsons. Perhaps you would explain yourself?' Mr. Saunders was brisk and business-like.

'I went to the aerodrome to meet my cousin. He had been to the funeral of a family friend, sir.'

'He took all night to tell you about it?'

'No, sir.' Christina felt herself blushing. 'I'm sorry, sir, I did not mean to be late back, but he—he had some work to do on one of the machines and I stayed to—to help him.'

'All night!' The words burst from Mrs. Carter's lips with a venom that frightened Christina. 'You stayed with him all night?'

'Until three o'clock, working.'

'Just the two of you?'

'Yes, but we—'

'You're shameless!' Mrs. Carter's face was taut with disgust. Two bright spots of colour glowed in her cheeks. 'You've the impudence to stand there and tell Mr. Saunders that you have spent the night alone with a man! You're not *ashamed* to tell him? You've the—'

'I've nothing to be ashamed about,' Christina said, and at the same time she felt her cheeks burning with what felt like shame. She was horrified by Mrs. Carter's outburst. 'It wasn't what you are thin—'

56

'I know how you young girls carry on these days! You don't have to explain to me. You're fast and immoral! I won't answer for her, Mr. Saunders, if she stays. I think Mrs. Marchant should be told at once.'

'Mrs. Marchant knows Will,' Christina burst out. 'He is her nephew—we are cousins. We—'

'She will be doubly horrified, in that case,' Mrs. Carter said tartly. 'No well-brought-up young man would compromise a girl in such a way—'

'But it wasn't me—it was the aeroplane he stayed up all night for!' Christina burst out. She felt the tears suddenly raining down her cheeks for the smashing of her bliss, the pounding in the mire of sensations so fragile and so perfect that Mrs. Carter in her piglike, bigoted rage could not even begin to conceive of them. 'You don't understand!' she cried out, the sobs hiccuping up.

'I understand all right, believe me, my girl! I know your sort. I wasn't born yesterday. I know what you were—'

'That's enough, Mrs. Carter,' Mr. Saunders put in suddenly. 'I don't think you need say any more.'

'You make it all dirty!' Christina sobbed, beside herself now with shock and exhaustion. 'It wasn't like that! It was—'

'Be quiet, girl,' said Mr. Saunders wearily. 'I promised your aunt, you know, that I would watch over your moral welfare. You understand that I cannot have you staying out all night, whatever you might or might not have been doing. You want to keep this job, don't you?'

'Yes, sir.'

The door opened suddenly and Dorothy put her head round. 'Mr. Marley wants a word with you, Dad.' She looked at Christina. 'Is anything wrong? Have I interrupted something?'

'No. Come in a moment,' her father said. 'Were you at the airfield last night? Did Christina go down with you?'

'No. Sandy came up here. He said she was there, helping Bill, because he had to change the warp wires on the Blériot before six o'clock this morning. Sandy said the work would take him all night, just about.'

'All right, Mrs. Carter, you may go now.' Mr. Saunders spoke

57

sharply to the housekeeper, as if Dorothy's evidence had closed the cross-examination. 'I will deal with Miss Parsons.' He waited until Mrs. Carter, with a vicious departing glance at Christina, had closed the door behind her, then said, 'Sit down, Christina, you silly girl, and stop crying. Mrs. Carter is only acting according to her conscience. We'll forget this little incident, if you just remember to behave in a more responsible manner in future.

Dorothy was laughing. 'Sandy said you'd be late. He said Bill would need someone at hand just to keep him awake, if the job was to get finished.'

Mr. Saunders got up from his desk, small and neat in his wide starched collar and well-cut suit. He looked at his daughter, vivid and conspicuous as usual in a dress of bright yellow shantung, and gave a small sigh.

'You girls—' he said, and stopped. It was evident that if he was troubled by anyone's behaviour, he was more troubled by Dorothy's than Christina's. 'Tell Mr. Marley I'll be with him directly, Dorothy.'

He turned to Christina and said, 'You've got sense. Just use it, and I'll forget all this. You've a good opportunity here if you want it. Miss Smithers tells me you're very quick in the office, and a great help to her. Perhaps it would be best if you stay there in future, and keep out of Mrs. Carter's province. Miss Smithers is anxious to leave, so as soon as she feels you can manage you can take on her job. Now go to bed and get some sleep, and be in the office at two o'clock. I will tell Mrs. Carter what I've decided. And, Christina—' He paused, as Christina rose to leave. 'Don't be led astray by Dorothy. The girl has no mother to advise her. I do my best, but I'm afraid I don't condone her behaviour, any more than I do yours. But she tells me I'm old-fashioned. Now run along.'

Christina went back to her room, shaken. She realized that the outcome of the interview was completely in her favour, but she was shattered by the despoiling of her precious experience, by the running amok of Mrs. Carter's dirty, common mind over the perfection of the summer night she had spent with Will. She drew the curtains in her small room, and lay on her bed and wept. . . .

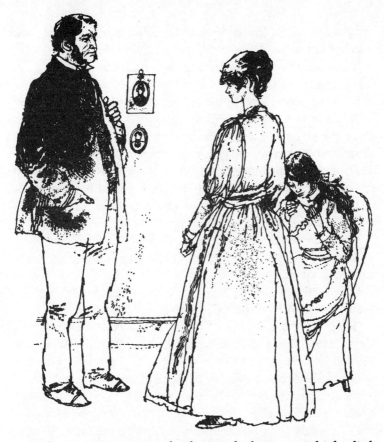

As the summer progressed, Christina had reason to think a little
bitterly at times that, if—in deference to Mrs. Carter—she had
stopped visiting Elm Park she would never have seen Will at all,
for he never left the confines of the aerodrome.

'Why do you work so hard?' she asked him.

'Because there is so much to do,' he said simply.

'Will there always be so much to do?'

'Not later on, perhaps.' He would smile at her, defying her to
be angry. 'Not when we're rich.' Did he ever think about her
when he was working, she wondered, as she thought about him
in Miss Smithers' office? She very much doubted it. Amongst the
mass of papers on his desk, covered in calculations and figures, there
were no absent-minded doodles of her profile, no elaborate hearts

entwined with the fine penline which alone had the power to set hers beating faster.

Since becoming the owner of *Emma*, he had had to hire a shed for her, and so had his own quarters, with slightly more room than in the other one. The shed cost him more than half his wages: hence his anxiety to get *Emma* flying again, so that he could make some money out of her. Mr. Adams had agreed to pay him more if the advanced pupils were given an opportunity to fly *Emma*, and William was rebuilding her with dual controls. He had made several radical alterations to her design, intended to improve her stability; he seemed to have no doubt, as he rebuilt her, that she would be an immensely better aircraft.

'But how do you *know*, until you fly her?' Christina asked.

'Because of all that, of course,' William replied, with a gesture towards his desk.

Christina was baffled. 'But if it is so easy, why don't all the machines fly? Why doesn't Raymond's, for example?'

'I didn't say it was easy, Christina, did I? You—of all people— know how long I've been trying to learn all this. Raymond's monstrosity is stressed all wrong. If it ever gets off the ground— which God forbid—it will fall to pieces in the air.'

Personal frustrations apart, it was entertaining to be accepted as a familiar of the airfield, for the atmosphere there was very much of the moment, compounded of a gay, reckless desire to be in on the new craze, a maniacal dedication to the mechanics of the thing, and all the shades between. Will was not alone in the serious business of getting a new machine to fly, nor Sandy in the happy-go-lucky, day-to-day business of earning a bit of cash. Mr. Dermot's erstwhile mechanic Joe, having arrived at Elm Park in the role of chauffeur for the purpose of delivering Sandy's motor-car, stayed on to take a job of mechanic to a young man called Freddie Pugh who kept a racing Deperdussin, and he spent all his spare time helping Will to rebuild *Emma*. When she visited Elm Park— nearly always with Dorothy—Christina used to love the hours when Will would at last tear himself away from the shed and come and join the others over the never-ending cups of tea on the café lawn, where the talk ranged over such topics as Mr. De Havilland's capturing the British height record, the fatal sideslip of Captain Loraine over Salisbury Plain, the flight by Commander Samson covering nearly two hundred miles without stopping and—incessantly—the fortunes of the competitors in the Military Trials that were taking place throughout August on Salisbury Plain. Christina would sit listening so that she knew the results, the disasters and the highlights by heart; she understood none of it, yet she could repeat the jargon and the figures and be perfectly happy watching Will letting his tea go cold while he pencilled explanatory diagrams on the tablecloth. Sandy would argue and behind his back Freddie would wink at Dorothy, and Dorothy would laugh and throw back her head. All the men joked and flirted with Dorothy and she loved it. Sandy would watch her, not saying anything, his face sometimes very serious.

When they had finished talking about the Trials, Will would say to Christina, 'Give me two years, and it will be my machine winning a competition like that, Christina, not Mr. Cody's mausoleum.'

'Four thousand pounds!' Christina said. 'That was a prize worth winning. If you had four thousand pounds you could do anything you wanted.'

'Yes, well, forty would do me for a start,' William said. 'As soon as *Emma* is flying we'll see if we can win a little something. I've got to have some money before I can start building my own machine.'

'Your winner?'

'Yes. The Russell world-beater. You know what, Christina, I'm going to call her the Dermot, after the old man. I owe everything to him, poor old beggar. You know—Joe told me—he took a little while over dying, and that's when he said give *Emma* to me. He made Joe write it down. Fancy bothering to think of that when—well, you know—' His voice dropped. 'He should never have tried to fly her. He never could fly.'

'I hope *you* can fly,' Christina said shakily.

'Of course I can fly, sweetheart. She's different now. I'll take you up in her as soon as she's ready, and you'll see how sweet she is.'

Christina, remembering that she did not fuss, stifled her instinctive protest.

Christina's greatest difficulty lay in finding the time to go and see Aunt Grace, which meant sacrificing a precious afternoon off. And when she was with Aunt Grace she had to be very careful what she said about her visits to the aerodrome, for she knew that Aunt Grace would never understand in a hundred years that visiting the aerodrome was not seemly behaviour without a chaperone. She would never understand, in her hidebound Victorian way, that on the aerodrome everyone was taken for granted if they were interested in the machines. There was no distinction of class or underdog; the mechanics, the pilots, the pupils and the owners all mingled without status. Brought up in what Christina now thought of as the medieval atmosphere of Flambards with its forelock-touching subservience on the part of the servants (and she remembered Dick—the groom who had suffered the most from this state of affairs—telling her that he could remember her Uncle Russell laying into his underlings with a hunting whip when he was angry), she looked on the way of life at Elm Park as the normal order of life. Aunt Grace would never understand this attitude.

On one of her visits, Christina was informed by Aunt Grace, 'Believe it or not, I've actually received a letter from your Uncle Russell. The first since he wrote to say Isobel had died—Will's mother, that is. And he says, dear child, as I've no doubt you might have guessed, that he will never give his consent to your marriage while there is breath in his body. Of course that only bears weight until you are both twenty-one, but even so, you had better resign yourself, Christina, to the knowledge.'

'Yes, Aunt Grace.' It meant very little to Christina just then for, with or without Russell's consent, marriage was impossible in their present circumstances. She concentrated on telling Aunt Grace about her progress under Miss Smithers, her speed with the typewriting machine and dexterity at the telephone switchboard, and the visits passed without incident.

Emma flew and, as predicted by Will's mathematics, was a

complete success. With a top speed of sixty-five miles per hour, she was the fastest machine on the field, after the French Deperdussin. Although no longer cranky, she was very sensitive to her controls, and had a high landing speed which invariably attracted

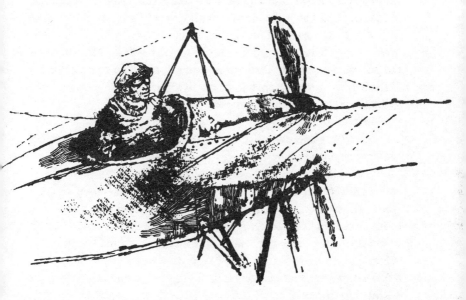

attention when she came in from a flight. Will, although pleased with her performance, was moody at this time. There was no jubilation in his manner when he climbed stiffly down from the cockpit in front of his own shed. He was quiet, often irritable, and looked tired and worried. Christina was familiar with his moods, and said nothing to him, but knew that it was no figment of her imagination. She knew that Sandy had lent him money to buy some of the materials he had needed for *Emma*, but she did not think debt was the cause of his troubles.

'Hasn't he offered you a ride yet, Christina?' Sandy asked her one afternoon. 'He's not very gallant these days, is he?'

Christina did not want to be asked, but it was a symptom of Will's malaise that he had not offered. Perversely, she would rather he had. 'There's plenty of time,' she said, not committing herself.

'She's a little beauty to fly,' Sandy said. 'Very tricksy. You can't sit up there dreaming. And a little devil to land. But very nice. He's a clever lad, your Will.'

'Oh, yes.' She accepted this fact. 'It doesn't seem to have made him very happy, though.'

Sandy frowned, and said nothing. Christina looked at him, and felt that Sandy at least knew what she was talking about.

'What's wrong with him?' she asked.

'Well—' Sandy leaned back on one of the long-suffering café chairs, tilting its legs. They were alone, Dorothy having gone for a flip with Freddie Pugh. Sandy was waiting for his next pupil and Will was refuelling the Farman.

'What is it?'

'I think it's because, now he's flying again, he realizes what he's up against with that leg.'

'Oh!' Having taken Will's own protestations about the ease with which he could fly *Emma* as gospel, Christina—amazingly, as she now realized—had never given this explanation a thought. 'But I thought he had arranged the controls so that he can manage?'

'Yes, he has, and devilish cunning it is too. But I've tried it, Christina, to see what it's like. I kept my leg stiff and pretended I was Will and believe me, even with his patent rudder control, it's damnably difficult.'

'But he always said it was all right. He's always managed up to now.'

'Well, I dare say he did when he started. Two or three years ago machines were very different from what they are today. But they're getting more sophisticated all the time, and *Emma* certainly requires a pilot who's a hundred per cent. I think Will's just discovered this. Before, he was so involved in building her that he never gave it a thought. Now, he's in the throes of realizing that flying is not for him.'

'Oh, no!' Christina looked at Sandy, appalled. 'But he's depending on flying to earn some money so that he can build his own—the Dermot! He was going to give flights, and Mr. Adams said he could do some instructing—and he was going to win some competitions—'

'Yes, he used to talk about competitions a good deal. But since he's been flying *Emma* I haven't heard him talk about it, have you?' Sandy's voice was gentle, but firm.

'No!' Sandy's home truths had hit Christina almost like a physical blow.

'Don't mention this to him, for heaven's sake,' Sandy added. 'It's only my guess. He hasn't said anything.'

'I'm sure you're right! I can't imagine why I never thought of it myself.' Christina rested her head in her hands, remembering Will all crumpled up on the sheep hurdle when the farm-hands had carried him into the house, Will saying he wanted to be a cripple so that he would never have to ride a horse again, Will walking on the broken bones against the doctor's orders. . . . No wonder he did not complain now, when she knew what he had done! Nobody knew but her. She did not need Sandy to tell her not to say anything.

Sandy got up from the table. 'There's my budding Blériot arriving. Pray for me, Christina! Will's losing nothing by not being an instructor—you take my word for it.'

Christina smiled automatically. Sandy bent down and said quietly, 'Don't worry. Will'll get by all right. He's got more aeronautical brains in his one head than all the other people on this field put together.'

But at the time this fact was no comfort to Christina.

On her last half day in September, Christina drove out to the aerodrome with Dorothy in Dorothy's new Ford, which her father had given her for her birthday. They were full of giggles at the novelty of it; everyone stared at them, the men whistled, and Christina pushed the thought of Aunt Grace right out of her head.

When they got to the aerodrome Sandy and Joe and Freddie were coming up to the café. When they saw the girls they did not greet them in their usual off-hand cheerful way, but they all looked grave, almost sheepish, and Christina saw Sandy and Freddie exchange glances in a way that gave her an unexpected qualm in the stomach.

'My, you're very serious today,' Dorothy said happily. 'What's wrong with you?'

'Where's Will?' Christina asked.

There was a short silence, and the three men all looked at Christina with their worried, embarrassed faces.

'He's gone away,' Sandy said awkwardly. 'In *Emma*,' he added.

'Where to? To Essex?' Christina was baffled by their strange reluctance. 'There's nothing wrong?'

Sandy cleared his throat nervously. 'Well, not really. It's just that he's gone to — to Switzerland.'

Chapter 7

The next three months seemed to Christina the longest of her life. It appeared that the only person who had had any previous idea of what William was going to do was Joe, because, being under-occupied with looking after the single machine of his own employer, he was going to do Will's work while he was away.

'And it wasn't any good trying to put him off the idea,' he explained to Christina. 'You know how he is when he wants to do something.'

Yes, Christina thought, she knew. Stubbornness ran in the Russell family. They all wanted their own way, and that was why at Flambards there had always been sparks flying.

'But will he get there safely? It's a terrible journey! He's never done any long-distance flying.'

But all the boys assured her that there was no reason why he should not arrive safely, in time. They pointed out that there was a good railway line to follow all the way.

'If he goes via Amiens and Reims, he'll pick up the line from Paris to Basle. And they say in France there is nearly always somewhere to land if you want it—it's not all chopped up into little fields like England.'

'And what about the Channel?'

'Oh, it's been crossed quite a few times this year. Hamel's been over three times! It's not dangerous in clear weather, Christina, as long as the old engine doesn't pack up. And you can be sure Will would see that that was in order before he set off.'

Nevertheless, Christina was not the only one waiting for the assurance of a letter in the familiar rapid handwriting. Christina read Mr. Saunders' *Times* avidly every morning to see if any aviation accidents were reported in the European news, and prayed avidly at her bedside every evening for Will's safe deliverance. It was fourteen days before a letter came, addressed to her at 'The Bunch of Grapes'. When she came across it, opening the mail in her little office with Miss Smithers, she excused herself hastily and ran with it to the privacy of the bathroom, locking the door behind her.

Four pages of the letter described the flight and one half-page spoke briefly of his present circumstances.

'I have made friends with the gardener in the clinic where this doctor works. He is very kind and lets me sleep in his shed. The doctor is very busy and says (I think, as he only speaks German) that he cannot see me, so I sit in the hallway of the clinic all day. It is a narrow hallway, and everyone falls over my leg, including Herr Doktor four times a day, once in the morning, twice at lunchtime, and once in the evening. I think sooner or later he will do something about it. Tell Sandy the nurses here are like Amazons. They can pick grown men up with one arm.'

It was apparent that he did not imagine that Christina was worrying over him.

'Oh, he thinks I am calm and sensible! He thinks I don't fuss!' Christina told herself, in despair. 'If he could see me—like a madwoman!' She wept a little, then went back to Miss Smithers, hoping no one would notice her red nose. In the evening Sandy came up and read the letter, absorbed by the four pages of graphic incident. Christina was already wondering how Will intended to pay for his treatment.

'*Emma* is worth around a thousand pounds,' Sandy commented. 'He's not really destitute any longer. Perhaps he'll offer Herr Doktor a part-share.'

'He can hardly fly back in half an aeroplane!'

Sandy grinned. 'Perhaps Herr Doktor will do it for the advancement of aviation.'

Ten days later another letter came. It was brief. 'Herr Doktor has capitulated. Today one of the Amazons came down to the hall and gave a rather nasty nut-cracking sort of mime and said, "Tomorrow 'e bend you." So if I don't write again for a bit don't worry. *Emma* has been damaged by cows, but it is not too bad.'

68

Christina did not know whether to be elated or petrified by this news. Already, by the time she received the letter, Will would be either on the road to recovery, or dying of blood-poisoning. 'Do not fuss!' she said to herself, reading and re-reading the brief sentences. Each day passed like a week. She heard nothing. 'If he has died, they must tell his father, and I would hear!' she thought frantically. She was sure that the methodical German Amazons would have taken the trouble to note down his next of kin before they started work. Germans were like that, not like the happy-go-lucky French. She lost her appetite. The weather grew cold, and the newspapers were full of the news of the tragic deaths of the pilots of two new monoplanes, one of which stalled when its engine failed, the other breaking up in the air. Christina thought of the long, cold journey home from Switzerland, and the crossing of the winter Channel.

'Flying is easier in the winter,' Sandy tried to comfort her. 'The air is much smoother.'

'Oh, yes,' Christina said sarcastically. She read from the newspaper on her desk: 'The machine was seen to glide down from 500 to 400 feet, and then rise again. At that moment both wings collapsed, and the machine fell in scattered pieces, with no chance of survival for Edward Petre.'

'Come to the movies with us, Christina,' Sandy said. 'We're going to see Charlie Chaplin at the Super Cinema.'

He was waiting for Dorothy, with his Ford Model T in the road outside. It was Christmas; the hotel was busy, and Christina was glad, for there was nowhere for her to go, and no one for her to spend it with, Aunt Grace having gone away with a friend.

'No, I've no time off tonight. It's all right, Sandy, I'm not fussing. I'm sorry. I've got stacks of work to do.'

She was ashamed of her fears. When Sandy and Dorothy had gone she looked again at the Christmas card she had received from Mark, the first communication from Flambards since she had left. Mark, in his usual insensitive way, was obviously not much put out, in retrospect, by her defection. His message was cheerful. The card showed a hectic hunting scene, and inside, in Mark's awful handwriting, was written: 'Good season so far. Boxing

Day meet here as usual. Drummer misses you. Father is putting him up for sale.' Christina stared at the card, her feelings a miserable tangle of anxiety, loneliness and homesickness, dashed with a pang of grief for gallant little Drummer, eager and yet gentle. Yet she knew there was nothing she would have changed, and so was angry with herself for being miserable.

Three weeks later she was reading of another flying tragedy: 'At the inquest, seizure of the engine was given as the cause, the cold weather having obstructed the supply of oil.' There was still no word from Will. 'They have killed him,' Christina wept to herself. 'If not that German doctor, then *Emma*. . . .'

Another three weeks dragged past. Christina was in the back office checking a list of figures from the butcher when Miss Smithers put her head in and said, 'Attend to the gentleman at the counter, Christina, I'm on the telephone.' Christina, memorizing 'Two pounds, twelve and sixpence', went automatically into the reception.

'Dinner for two, please,' said the gentleman. 'A celebration dinner.'

Christina stood rooted, unable to speak. She felt as if her heart had suddenly swollen up, pressing all the breath out of her, as if her blood had evaporated completely.

'*Will*!'

He was all smiles, pink and healthy-looking, not drowned or mangled or dying at all . . . *real* . . .

'It's you, Will—'

'The one and only real, bending William Russell,' he agreed.

'It's all right? You—you—is it?'

'Yes, it's all right, God bless the Herr Doktor. Look, you haven't got to work, have you? I want to take you out to dinner. I've got Sandy's car outside.'

'Oh, Will!'

'I mustn't fuss,' Christina thought, but there were black spots before her eyes. Everything happened in a dream. The butcher's bill . . . 'Have a sniff of this, you do look queer,' in an undertone from Miss Smithers . . . 'Of course, take the rest of the evening off,' from Mr. Saunders, all jovial and hand-shaking with Will at the bar. 'You can borrow my fur tie, if you like,' from Dorothy. Then they were driving through the rain . . . a little place by the river with a table in an alcove and red velvet seats, and candlelight, like a dream, like one of old Mary's romantic novels . . . stars in her eyes, thought Christina, and all that rubbish, and Will all handsome and smiling . . . *alive* . . .

'I thought you were dead!'

'But I wrote, when I knew I could leave. Didn't you get it?'

'Not since you said he was going to do it. Nothing.'

'Oh, Christina, I'm sorry! That was ages ago. I gave my letter to Ingrid—Ingrid the Amazon—I suppose she never bothered—'

'It's been like four years, not four months!'

'Don't tell me, I know! I know I was keen to get in, but then when I was in I thought I was going to be there for life. He's a real perfectionist, I'll give him that, the Herr Doktor. A real engineer. Just like working on an old crate really, getting it to go again . . . I can see the satisfaction. But day after day after day, just lying there and nothing to do, and worrying about *Emma*! She was on a farm, I managed to bring her down in this big cow-pasture. Of course there was no shed for her. I had to work on her for a solid week before I could leave, and I only had bits of spares, and no cash. It was all makeshift, botching up, but the best I could do. I wanted all the money I had for fuel. Lord, Christina, I've got to earn some money now! I owe the doctor three hundred pounds for that operation. I could sell *Emma* and pay him, but on the other hand, she is my only opportunity of making money. I thought I'd give competitive flying a go this coming season, and anything I can work out that could bring in the cash, and if it's no good, and I'm a failure—well, then I could sell *Emma* and pay him. If the worst comes to the worst, so to speak. But I don't see why it should! I'm sure I can make a go of it now. And the difference it makes to flying, Christina—it was worth every bit of all the misery, ten times over! Lord, I'm lucky.'

'I've saved some money. Five pounds. You can have that.'

'No, don't worry. I'm sure I can earn it all right, Christina. There are all sorts of ways now—races across the Channel and . . .' Christina watched him, not worrying about what he was saying in the light of her bliss in merely having him before her eyes. 'Races across the Channel . . .' It meant nothing to her now that he was not dead. It was far in the capricious future, not to be considered when they were safe in the velvet hotel with glasses of champagne. She could not take her eyes off him. 'He must not know how I wept and carried on,' she thought. 'Oh, I can be calm and cool now! I have nothing to worry about!' The champagne made the room go round, so that all she could see properly was the candle-flame reflected in Will's eyes across the table, and she remembered Aunt Grace writing in a letter, long ago it seemed, 'Do not drink too much, Christina, it is very unseemly and can get you into bad trouble.' And now here she was, dining alone with a young man in public, and all her brain full of love and champagne. She was wicked, and her reputation was all in ruins, but she did not care.

'I kept thinking you must have died!' She could laugh now. 'I thought they had killed you, and didn't know who you were, and I should never know!'

Will laughed. It was very easy to laugh now, but probably, Christina thought shakily, Will hadn't laughed very much during the last four months either.

And then the evening was over, and everything was back to normal again, with the first flickering scent of spring in the air, and Will's path smooth, at last, for doing what he wanted.

'Whatever is that?'

Christina stood on the beaten track that ran down to the sheds and looked up as a glint of sunlight on an object high up in the sky caught her eye. It was too high to make out properly, but appeared to be coming down—whatever it was—vertically.

'Is something wrong?' she said to Sandy sharply.

'No,' Sandy said, pausing to watch.

'Gracious, I never know,' Christina apologized. How could one tell? she wondered. She could see now that the object was a monoplane descending in a very tight corkscrew spiral, its circles appearing to be not a lot more in diameter than the length of the plane. It appeared to be spinning round on one wing-tip. Its rate of fall made Christina's flesh come up in goose-pimples. But she knew she must keep very calm.

'It's—' she cleared her throat. 'It's Will, isn't it?'

Sandy grinned at her, sideways. 'Well—could be—'

'It looks awful.' She couldn't help it.

'The idea is to pull out before you hit the ground,' Sandy said comfortably.

'But you must get dizzy.' It was an effort to keep her voice merely conversational.

'You get used to it,' Sandy said, still unperturbed.

Would *she* ever? Christina wondered. But she did not scream, or even turn her eyes away. She compelled herself to go on looking, and saw the little plane come cleanly out of its spiral some fifty feet from the ground, the horrid whine giving way to the sudden roar of its engine. It whistled across the field, and over the boundary trees in a steeply banked turn. Christina let out her breath in a short, angry sigh. By the time *Emma* had returned, landing into the wind with her usual hair-raising impetuosity, she was nonchalent and cheerful. Will had the grace to look slightly sheepish when he saw her.

'You're early,' he said. 'I was going to be waiting for you, all clean and tidy, like a proper gent.'

'Miss Smithers let me go before lunch—we hadn't much to do.'

'Good. Because Sandy's going to lend me his motor-car— aren't you, Sandy?—so that we can go for a little spin. So we'll have a couple of hours—' he glanced at Sandy's watch— 'before I've got to be back. I've got a pupil at four.'

'You see?' Sandy said to Christina. 'First my motor-car, now my pupils. You've really got to watch this rotter.'

Christina laughed. 'I can't imagine any pupils trusting their lives to him!'

'No, well, to be truthful, it's invariably the other way round, Christina. He's just finding out, now Mr. Adams has advanced his status to instructor. He comes down all green and trembling.'

'By jiminy, you're right. If it wasn't that it meant three pounds a week I'd go back to being a mechanic.'

'Are there enough pupils for both of you?'

'Yes, we have a waiting list!' Sandy said. 'We're such popular boys, you understand. And if there wasn't a waiting list, I'd have seen to it by now that Will was out on his ear. I knew he was after my job the moment I set eyes on him swigging tea in the café.'

The arrival of Sandy's pupil terminated the banter. Will changed out of his flying gear, fetched Sandy's motor-car, and soon they were bowling out of the gates and across the heather-covered common. After Will's former dedication to his work, Christina found the fact that he could now take a couple of hours off to entertain her very encouraging. She knew that it would only last until he started work building his new machine, the Dermot; and he would not do that until he had earned some money to buy the materials.

They stopped near a big pond that lay a few hundred yards off the road, surrounded by pine-trees. It was a popular spot with motor-car enthusiasts in the summer, according to Sandy, when it was used for swimming and picnic parties. Now, a weekday in March, it was deserted. A warm sun was drawing out all the scents of the resinous needles underfoot and the pungency of the still green water; a few ants ran over the sandy paths. It was a place to ride a horse, Christina thought, the hooves silent on the thin soil.

'It's a bit different from Flambards' covert,' she said, thinking of the deep, dark clay and the brimming Essex ditches. 'Look! Down there—quite big fish—'

In the shadow of the overhanging pines a shoal of fish swam lazily, by some trick of the light very conspicuous. One, larger than the rest, came up to the surface and turned over with a flick of its tail, showing a pale belly, then sank down again, rolling over, as if swimming for the sensuous joy of it. It could turn all ways without effort, twisting and turning. They stood watching until Christina, bored, turned away, kicking up the sand. They walked on along the track beside the pond, and Will said, 'That fish—in its element—is how an aircraft should be in the sky. One day an aircraft will be flown the way that fish swam in the water.'

'But the fish turned right over on its back.'

'Yes, that's what I mean.'

'Oh, Will! Surely not! What would happen to the poor pilot?'

'He would be strapped in, idiot child. And he would see the horizon come up over his head, and the earth spinning round on the tip of his wing, and the sky below him, and all the time he would not worry, because the aircraft would fly like the fish swam.'

Christina looked sideways at Will walking along with his hands behind his back. He kicked at the sand and watched the little spurts of dust spray out before him. He had taken his cap off and his black hair flopped from his parting over his forehead, and his eyes were thoughtful, watching the dust. Christina sighed to herself, aware that she had lost him for the time being. He slipped through her fingers like the fish in the water, and she could only wait.

'We've scarcely started yet,' he said.

What did he see? Christina wondered. She saw only the danger. He saw the stars and the moon, and space without end. She lifted up her face to the sun and loved the outdoors, with her feet on the ground, after all the days in the stuffy hotel. It was all she wanted, the smell of the pines, and Will walking beside her, with her in body if not in spirit. She loved the way he walked now, with a faint click in his knee at intervals, and a slight limp, as if he did not wholly trust the new machinery. The stiff leg had been such a characteristic part of Will ever since she had known him that she still could not get over the sense of shock every time she met him.

Will's dreams were giving place to reality. 'Listen, Christina, I have something wonderful to tell you. I kept it back, till we were in a nice place, because it is such a lovely piece of news.'

Christina stopped and stared at him. 'What is it?' Her mind raced, trying to think of wonderful pieces of news. Stupidly, and with an underlying sense of horror at her wickedness in thinking it, the only thing that came to mind was the death of her Uncle Russell, Will's father.

'I have been offered fifty pounds for doing a delivery job for Mr. Foulkes-Parker—you know, that chap with the big blond moustache, more money than sense.' (Christina let out her breath in a quick sigh, half relief, half disappointment.) 'He has a two-seater Blériot that he wants flying back to Blériot's works. He's bought a new model with a bigger engine, and the idea is that I fly the old one over and bring the new one back. And as it's a two-seater, Christina, I thought you would come along too. You said you had a week-end off due to you. It would be the most terrific fun—and fifty pounds! What an opportunity!'

'But Blériot's works are—' Christina cleared her throat, to steady her voice. She started again, very softly, to stop the panic. 'It means crossing the Channel.'

'That's the point, sweetheart! It was so wonderful before: I couldn't describe it to you—I would give anything for you to see it. We would choose our weather, of course—we wouldn't do anything stupid, so you needn't be afraid. We could do it there and back in a day if we were lucky. One hop to Dover, and another to Hardelot—which is right on the beach on the other side, just round Gris-Nez. There's nothing to it in a good machine, given the weather, Christina.'

Will's eyes were shining at the mere thought of it. He was all animation and excitement. Christina could not help but laugh at him, although her insides were cold with despair. 'I will not think about it,' she thought to herself. 'Not until it happens . . .'

'It's time you had a bit of fun, working in that doss-house of Dorothy's all the time. It'll give you something to look forward to. You're a marvellous girl, Christina. I mean, I can ask you— you're the sort. Lots of sense. Not all giggles and blinking your eyelashes like Dorothy.'

'Dorothy wouldn't mind flying the Channel,' Christina said instantly.

'Not if there was a man involved, no,' Will agreed. 'But you don't mind, surely?'

'Not if there's a man involved,' Christina said smoothly.

Will laughed delightedly. 'Any old man?'

'Any *young* man. Preferably with a knee that clicks.'

Will laughed again. He was full of spirits, like a boy, and Christina had to laugh too. It wasn't a day for worrying. They ran back to Sandy's motor, and Will gave her a driving lesson down the sandy tracks, and they laughed helplessly, until the tears ran down their faces. Then it was time for Will to go back.

The afternoon had been marvellous, but Christina knew that there was this thing ahead of her, that she did not dare think about. It was like a great black tunnel on her railway track, and she racing towards it at eighty miles an hour, but trying to pretend it wasn't going to happen. She could not get to sleep that night, and when she did, she had nightmares that—when she woke up—she could not remember.

CHAPTER 8

It seemed to Christina fantastic that William, clever as he was, did not perceive her true feelings about flying the Channel. The night before, unable to eat, she had been literally sick with fear. Dorothy, thinking she had an upset stomach, gave her some pills 'to settle it'. But nothing, Christina knew, would settle what she was suffering from. And almost as strong as this abject fear was this feeling of amazement that William did not see it, this daze of acting a part that she was able to perform so convincingly, smiling blindly as she put on the ghastly clothes that Dorothy had assembled for her, even laughing outside the shed. The nightmare had taken hold so strongly that she felt almost as if it were someone else being so normal, winding this horrid woollen hood round her head and tucking the ends down over her chest, buttoning up the thick leather coat; it was some friend of hers going on this flight and she herself was watching her go. It was only when she turned back into the shed to get herself a pair of goggles that she caught Sandy's eye, and she knew then that Sandy was not deceived. He, the only one of them all, knew what she was really feeling. He gave her a small sympathetic smile, and a quick wink, and she felt comforted out of all proportion.

The two-seater Blériot was very small, a papery, spidery-looking contraption with its single wing and squarely-set landing wheels guyed by a conglomeration of wires. When she was in her passenger seat Christina was open to the elements from the waist up. Behind her the fuselage was not even covered over with fabric, but was a bare skeleton of bolted struts and more wire. After the stately Farman with the great umbrella of its top wing stretched over one's head and the lower wing spread out on either hand in comforting abundance, sitting in the Blériot was like being perched on the back of a flea.

William, true to his promise, had chosen a day of fine, settled weather. They started early, as soon as it was light, the machine climbing neatly and surely away from the small knot of people by the shed, Christina peering, teeth shut tight, at the disappearing ground, the map-like striations of road and railway, pond blob and orchard sprawl, thin blue smoke and the green fuzz of sprouting corn. Because of what was to come, this was only mildly terrifying, and quite bearable. She had flown several times with Will now, never without feelings of great reluctance, always in the vicinity of the aerodrome. She was familiar now with this fantastic feel of separation from the earth, the other-worldliness of this new sphere; she could appreciate the boys' delight in riding these unnatural craft, but knew that this element was not for her. She had taken the controls in *Emma* once or twice, feeling Will's hands on the dual; when he had taken them off, raising them in the air to show her, she had screamed, but in the din Will had not heard her. She flooded with shame when she thought of these things. She thought she ought to be able to laugh, but she couldn't. 'I don't have to like it,' she thought. 'There are no laws about it. And look what Will did to get out of riding horses! He ought to understand.' But he didn't even know. She sat in her cramped space, gradually getting colder and colder, watching the sun filling the sky all round her, licking the flicks of oil on her lips, watching the back of Will's head, loving and hating him, shivering. Once, with a terrible pang, she thought of Aunt Grace.

It was impossible to speak above the noise of the engine, and Will had a pad of paper on which he occasionally wrote notes and passed back to her. Christina was supposed to be keeping a log. Will handed back to her the names of the places they passed and she wrote them down with a note of the time. He then passed her, 'Speed?' and she had to study her map diligently to find the mileage, and work it out, which took her ages. Her first sum gave her four hundred and eighty miles per hour, which she had already written down ready to pass to Will before it struck her as odd. Muttering and fumbling, she tried again. Her fingers were numb with cold and her brain seemed equally addled. Her next result was fifteen miles per hour, but her third was sixty-eight, which she considered feasible and passed on. Will passed back, 'Wind helping. Happy?' 'Yes,' she returned. 'How strange,' she thought, 'to be talking to him on bits of paper, two thousand feet up in the sky.' She could have touched his cheek with her hand if she had wished, and below them all the while the great purple haze that was London drifted on the left wing-tip, shimmering with a sulphurous cloak of its own making. Deep inside it, Christina remembered, was Battersea, and Aunt Grace would be answering the door to Mrs. Astley, not knowing that her own flesh and blood were looking down on her like guardian angels. Christina, in spite of everything, had to laugh at this great unreality. It was true that descriptions could not do anything. She could not write, 'Dear Aunt Grace, I was in the sky and I saw . . .' Will had always said that he could not tell her what it was like, and now she knew why. Her sensations were not compounded of anything that words could do. She could never tell Aunt Grace.

Will passed back, 'Thames', jabbing his finger, and out of the haze she saw a silver thread looping, widening, spreading into a vague white mist which she supposed was the sea. 'Not our sea, thank God,' she thought. 'Not yet.' This was the Thames estuary, with the thick clay of Essex on the far shore. Her own sea, the Channel, was faintly visible far to the south, but Christina had no wish to look that way. First there was Eastchurch, on the Isle of Sheppey, where Will had promised to land for breakfast, and Christina had no wish to look beyond her breakfast.

The journey to Eastchurch took just under the hour, which seemed to satisfy Will. He brought the Blériot down close by the sheds, very neatly so that it stopped almost as soon as it touched, and Christina sat appreciating the beauty of mere silence, which she had never considered before. Sheppey was marsh country, with plovers tumbling about with their haphazard squeaks, and a curlew crying sadly as it winged its way over the ditches. Their voices, thin and clear, were lovely music in Christina's ears. She stumbled numbly out of her cramped seat, and Will held out a hand to her as she jumped down.

'Oh! Ugh!' She was so cold she could not feel herself. Will was grinning at her, his goggles pushed up, his face all smeared with oil.

'You di—dirty thing!' she said.

'You're not exactly lily-white yourself, sweetheart. The Gnome is notoriously generous with its oil—one and a half gallons an hour, mostly over the pilot. That was a good flight, eh? Perfect conditions. Let's get stoked up and push on while it holds. Oh, this is the life, Christina! All this and getting paid for the privilege! Aren't you glad you came?'

She nodded, because now that she was on the ground again it was perfectly true. She did not want to be anywhere else. Will was talking to the mechanics, shaking hands with somebody. Someone was talking to her, but her ears weren't functioning properly yet. Then she had a wash, quickly, and there were bacon and eggs and hot tea, gorgeous hot tea, and young men like Sandy and Freddie talking to Will about revs per minute and overheating, and Will talking earnestly back, laughing, eating, and she accepted as one of the party, smiling stiffly, warming her hands round the big tea mug, pretending that there was nothing to worry about.

In less than an hour they were off again, skimming over the bumpy marsh. The aircraft had been refuelled, and Will had peered at all the important parts, and tinkered with the engine for some minutes, while Christina had arranged her maps and her writing-pad. Then the shattering din once more, and the feel of the sky in her stomach, mixing uneasily with her breakfast. She was on her own again, riding with her own emotions. She could weep, or scream and nobody would know. She could laugh and sing, and no one would hear. She comforted herself with the thought of the landing at Dover which Will had promised. 'There's no need to be frightened yet.'

Some cloud had come up from the west, but was high up, a drifting white fleece. As they gained height, heading south-west, the whole corner of England was opened up to Christina's gaze, edged in soft silver from the Thames behind them to the infinity over the right wing-tip. Below there was apple blossom, and drifts of smoke going towards the east, and the neat sprawl that was Ashford, a glint of the Stour, the rolling patchwork of the downs and the white sheep scattered like bread to the birds. Higher, and colder, and the silver before them spread, shimmering, and the fleecy clouds imperceptibly drifted . . . Christina was hypnotized. 'Dear Aunt Grace,' her mind was saying stupidly, 'I was in the sky and I saw—' and then there was this impossibility again, this blockage.

The engine stopped and Christina was snapped into panic at the shock of it. Instead of the cracking din, there was a new sound of wind in the wires, a shrieking music that she had never heard before. And out of it, Will's voice, perfectly audible: 'There's nothing wrong. I switched off so that we can talk for a moment.'

A great gulp of relief . . . Christina adjusted her face as Will glanced round.

'I think we might as well press straight on,' he was saying. 'We've plenty of fuel and she's running very sweetly. That's Dover below, so we're right on course. We've got to allow for a good deal of westerly drift with this wind—I want to keep plenty of height, which means more wind-force to reckon with. I'm going to fly south-west until we can see Blanc Nez. We'll land at Calais, then do the last hop to Boulogne. The compass is not behaving very well, but that's normal—with this visibility it doesn't matter.'

'The cloud is increasing.'

'Yes. One of the reasons for pressing on. It's good and high though. It won't worry us. All right?'

'Yes, whatever you say.' Very calm and cool, Christina was thinking, pressing her fingers tight together to stop their shaking.

'Our speed won't be so good as on the last leg, because of allowing for the beam wind. But we should make it in well under the hour.'

'Yes, all right.'

The engine broke into life once more, and Christina felt the machine galvanized into effort under her seat-bones, like a horse whipped out of a pleasant reverie. The nose lifted again, and the little craft altered course slightly so that she was heading straight out over the silver. Christina looked down with a feeling of desperation, and saw the last of the green downs and the dots that were sheep, the last homely chimney and strip of shingle catching the sun. A fishing trawler with red sails . . . 'Oh, God,' she prayed.

'Please, please, *please*—' She was trembling so much she thought she must be causing as much vibration as the engine. She tried to pretend it was the cold, and could almost convince herself, for every part of her flesh was like ice. 'I don't fuss,' she said to herself. 'Will says I don't fuss.' And she looked at the back of his head, mere brown leather in his flying helmet and muffler and as distant as the man in the moon, and she felt this violent love-hate again, that she should do this for him, that he should *ask* her. 'He is mad,' she thought, and she looked over her shoulder and saw the line of white cliffs stark and receding in the sunshine, the ultimate boundary of everything a normal person could expect to take for granted: ground under his feet and grass and . . . and *ground*. Christina almost choked with the bitterness of it, that Will who professed to love her should deprive her of such ordinary comforts. 'They are all mad,' she thought. 'All of them.' And her eyes fastened on the edge of the cockpit she sat in and the flimsy nest of struts and canvas that supported her, and the quivering wings, as frail as a butterfly's. It was a cockleshell of ridiculous, unnatural ideas, she thought, like riding a toy and expecting the elements to be kind to it: no sane person would ever contemplate such folly. And as her thoughts turned to the elements, the fleecy cloud at last caught up with the sun, and she saw this curtain of shadow racing across the sea, swallowing up the silver and the shimmer, turning it to lead. Behind, the white cliffs were suddenly extinguished like candles under a snuffer. It meant nothing, but it appalled her, as if all her dark, maniacal thoughts were being reflected in the atmosphere, as if Will would know what she was thinking by a change in the weather.

Now, as the Blériot drew steadily out over the grey platter of the Channel, Christina found herself listening intently to the noise of the engine, quivering for the slightest hesitation in this infernal row. As William had predicted, their progress was not very fast. She could judge by the occasional fishing-boat crawling below, and a white-sailed schooner beating down Channel. She watched their passage in an agony of impatience, and strained her eyes towards the haze where the French coast lay. The minutes on her borrowed watch passed with infinite pain, as if petrified by the unnatural atmosphere through which they passed. The white cliffs of England receded into a grey nothingness, but the French shore remained equally insubstantial, so that Christina knew that they were really alone, suspended in this strange arena of air and water like a Pacific albatross that wanted nothing else. To have left the land was bad enough, but to be without even the sight of it was agony to Christina. She sat stiff with fear, peering and listening and praying and looking at the time, and praying.

She was not sure, at first, whether by such acute attention to the sound of the engine her imagination was playing her tricks, but as the time dragged on she felt that the din had changed its key. It was rougher now. She listened intently, holding her breath, not trusting herself to judge. Her heart was banging away as roughly as the rotary itself. She saw Will move in front of her, lean forward and wipe something. She could not see properly. With shaking fingers she wrote on her pad, 'Is everything all right?' and pushed the piece of paper forward over Will's shoulder. He half-turned his head to read it, took it in his fingers and let it fly away in the slipstream. She saw his head nod. The engine missed a beat, then carried on, and Will made no communication nor indication that it meant anything. 'But it does mean something,' Christina thought, a great sweat of horror breaking out all over her. She was trembling too much to write anything else. She put her hands up to her mouth, and pressed them against her icy flesh, feeling them shake.

Will put up his hand again and turned the engine off. The nose dipped. Will turned his head and said, 'Oil pressure's very low. We've got a leak. Revs have dropped off, but we've got enough height to make it. Don't worry.' Then the engine burst into life once more, before Christina had any chance to make a reply. Will jabbed his left hand out over the side of the cockpit, pointing forward, and far away—impossibly far away—out of the haze a line of land was visible. Christina looked at it and groaned. She looked at her watch. It might have stopped, for all the useless crawling of its black hands. 'Now,' she thought, 'this is what I dreaded, this is what I knew it would be like. I knew, I knew I was right.'

84

It was as if the Blériot had six passengers up, instead of just herself. Little by little she lost height. Will made no more communications. Once Christina peered forward to look at the revolution indicator, and she saw that in the forward cockpit oil was spraying everywhere. The stench of it nauseated her, smoking in her nostrils. She looked towards the land, and it was no nearer, but the sea was coming nearer all the time, grey and sullen and hard like pewter, empty of any sign of life save a few gulls skimming low. She wanted Will to send her a message, to talk to her, but she knew that he was using all his attention to keep his height without stalling. It was like sewing with the cotton running out, she thought inconsequently. She did not think about what was going to happen, only she remembered that she had never fancied drowning as a death. 'Don't think about it,' she said to herself carefully, and her mind carefully went all round the looming subject, and fixed itself on the low, shining sliver of land ahead, obstinately distant.

The sea, as they came inevitably closer, resolved itself into waves and troughs. The metallic similies were lost in the reality of the stuff. There was nothing fanciful in its nature at close quarters. Christina looked over the side, down over the wings, and saw the restless, desultory heaving of the grey waves. There was no comfort there; they were heedless of her feelings, grey vultures, slip-slapping in an endless, pointless dance up and down the Channel. She looked at the back of Will's head, and pictured him disappearing under the grey waves, and the hot tears welled up inside her goggles so that she could no longer see. Better not to see, she thought, sniffing numbly, better never to think . . . 'Dear Aunt Grace, We are over the sea . . . Dear Aunt Grace, The sea is over us . . .'

The coarse roar of the engine opened up slightly, and the machine held her course some fifty feet over the surface of the water. The sun showed through for a few minutes, and Christina watched their shadow undulating below, imagining all the time that it was getting closer, reaching up for them. Ahead of them the sands of Calais stood out in a golden line; the sun shone on the white pencil of the lighthouse, and a tumble of red roofs.

'Surely,' Christina thought, 'they will see us now, and send a boat out if we fall in. . .' And all at once, she realized that they were not going to drown after all. She could see the beach, and a lazy white wave rolling in. The beach was enormous, pale and empty, with rolling dunes beyond. Will had his hand up and was passing her a slip of paper. It was black with oil and she could not see the scrawl on it until she had wiped her eyes inside her goggles. They were banking now, turning into the wind to make a landing, so that the wing-tip was inches from the water. Christina watched the water, and held up the little slip of paper, and when the aircraft straightened out and the sand ran clean and firm below the wing-tips, she read what Will had written. Splattered all over with oil, the message read, 'I love you'.

When the Blériot came to a standstill, people seemed to materialize out of the sand itself. Before Christina could get down, there were three men grinning and smiling at her, holding out their arms to help her. A man on a bicycle was shaking hands with Will and others were running towards them in all directions. She could not understand a word anyone said, but their intentions were obviously friendly. Shocked, frozen, and stupid with joy, she blinked and smiled and nodded her head, while Will discussed his problems with the man on the bicycle in a sort of pantomime. Because the man knew aeroplanes, their progress was utterly satisfactory. More cans of castor oil appeared as if by magic, and the bulb that had caused the trouble was replaced. Will's clothes were saturated with oil, his cockpit was running with it.

'*D'où venez-vous? Et où allez-vous?*'

'*A Monsieur Blériot,*' Will said to the man on the bicycle, and everyone said, '*Ah, mais oui! A Monsieur Blériot!*' and when Will was satisfied with his engine once more, the two of them were helped in and their hands shaken with this heart-warming enthusiasm. Even Christina had to smile again, looking at the crowd all jostling to help manoeuvre the craft under the direction of the bicycle man. Will's face was alarmed for a moment at the pressure on the tail, but the bicycle man harangued the crowd and shouted assurances to Will. He swung the propeller, and the crowd roared '*Bon voyage*' and Will was shouting '*Merci, merci beaucoup!*'

above the din. Christina saw the sand racing past again, and the dust whirling off the dunes, waving hands and the waves rolling in under their spinning wheels. 'Again, again,' she thought. She felt exhausted by her emotions.

But the flight to Hardelot-Plage was uneventful, save for some bumpy air over the cliffs. The sun came out again, and the empty rolling downs gave way to Boulogne harbour, and then there was country of rolling dunes and pine-trees and another long stretch of firm sand to land on. When she climbed down this time, Christina felt like a veteran.

This time the Frenchmen were less excited, but no less welcoming. Christina's head ached violently. Will was quite happy indulging in the strange Anglo-French conversation that immediately ensued, making descriptive Gallic gestures with the best of them, but Christina slipped away, quite unable to face the gabbledegook —even in English she did not understand it. She threw off her heavy clothes and unwound the mufflers and left them lying in a heap on the sand, then walked away down the empty beach, pulling the hairpins out of her tangled, aching head until her hair fell loose, feeling the sun warm through her blouse and smelling the scent of inland heather and pine like balm on the air. She found she was crying again, because of the smell, and the ground under her feet, and she pulled herself up and wiped her eyes severely. 'It's the shock,' she thought. Not so much the shock of nearly being drowned, but the shock of still being alive. 'Oh, you fool! You fool!' she scolded herself, and she flung herself down on the warm sand where it gave way to dunes springy with rough grass and lay on her back with her face to the sun, listening to the silence. She was utterly content, back with the ground. She thumped it with her fists, hard and warm, and thought of it deep below her, on and on, firm and deep to the other side of the world. 'Oh, Will, why do I love you so, when you are so mad?' she wondered, and she held out the little scrap of paper he had passed to her, all covered with oil, with 'I love you' written on it, and laid it in the sun to get dried out, with a pebble on each corner to anchor it. It was only the second time he had ever told her this, the first time being at Badstocks the night they had run away. Now she had it in writing.

She lay luxuriously, aware of every ant, of every blade of grass that moved in the breeze. This was paradise, the sea far away down acres of warm sand. Behind, miles of rolling heather, and the valley of a lazy river running in, and hill-sides covered in pines. Her hair was full of sand; the ants ran over her bare arms. 'I could be happy for ever here,' she thought, but she knew she had only minutes. If it wasn't for Will, she thought, she would not ever have to be afraid, grovelling for courage with so little success. She could carry on in a perfectly ordinary way like everyone else did, in Kingston-on-Thames, and Essex, riding a bicycle if she wanted a little excitement, sleeping soundly at night.

'Christina!'

She sat up. Will was coming along the beach, tracking her footsteps. She sat up, pushed the oily note into her skirt pocket, and went to meet him.

'They've laid on a meal for us. The new machine's not quite ready yet, so there's no hurry. What are you doing? Sunbathing?'

'Just hugging the ground.'

Will grinned. 'I'm sorry if you had a scare. It was bad for the bulb to break—not as if we'd gone up to ten thousand feet or anything, when you might expect it. You weren't too worried, though, were you? Not you,' he added—as if she were Queen Victoria, Christina thought.

'Oh, no,' she said lightly. 'I love swimming.'

They walked back along the beach, oily hand in oily hand. 'You look lovely, all hairy,' Will said. 'And you, all oily,' Christina said back. His shoes squelched with it. 'You're pretty oily yourself, but I was too much of a gentleman to remark on it. I could have said, "You look lovely, all hairy and oily".' 'Sandy and hairy and oily,' Christina said. 'And hungry,' Will said. 'Hungry and sandy and hairy and oily.'

The new machine was not ready until four o'clock in the afternoon, by which time the sky had clouded over slightly, and Christina's stomach had contracted again. Will took the machine up for a trial flight while she wound up her hair again and buttoned herself back into her flying clothes. There was no argument against not going, for the visibility was good, and the wind light. The French mechanics were very kind, making gallant remarks (she thought), to which she had to smile back, although her smile already had the frozen feel about it that she could remember sensing before. She had to stand there, waiting, being calm, loathing every slow minute. But all was well. Will was very happy with the new machine; they said good-bye and shook hands all round, and then they were away once more, heading for Calais.

This time the crossing was uneventful, although the weather rapidly deteriorated as they reached the English coast. The cloud came lower, no longer fleecy, but grey and miserable-looking, pushed by an increasing wind. It was April weather, the sun skimming over green downs and disappearing into darkness, a white house almost flashing here and there, and the shadows running like galloping horses. Christina could feel the aircraft buffeted by the wind like a ship by green seas. It lurched and rolled, and she held on to the sides of the cockpit in horror, never having realized before that such things went on up aloft. Will had no hands to pass notes with, fully occupied with keeping the machine on a level keel, but Christina had to do her best with her maps, peering and checking and trying to ignore the awful nausea in her stomach. At Ashford there were two railway lines and two rivers, and innumerable shining streams to confuse. The machine dropped twenty feet like a stone and she almost lost the map, and certainly her dinner, moaning over the side of the cockpit. The compass needle was going round in circles. A town appeared below, and she was forced to write, 'Tonbridge or Maidstone?' but as she passed the note over Will's shoulder the cloud blotted out the whole landscape and Will put the nose down and started to glide down. The rain stung Christina's face, hammering on the fuse-lage and wings with a noise like a drum to accompany the scream-ing of the wires. Will shouted over his shoulder, 'We'll have to find somewhere to land when the squall's over. It'll be dark soon. Look out for a good place!' He had pushed his goggles up in order to see, and the rain was pouring over him as if they were under a waterfall. Christina could feel it going through her scarves and trickling down her neck. She peered over the side of the cock-pit, moaning softly with all this new misery, and saw the ground blurry and swirling below, all woods and hedges and lumps and clutter. Will flattened out and they flew on beneath the fringes of the cloud, the rain like ice needles darting into the skin. For a moment the setting sun shone wildly in their faces, all amongst the rain, so that the wings suddenly looked like flames dancing with water. Then a black cloud shut it out, and Christina realized that the day was finished. The ground was grey and disappearing, a light shining here and there, and they were marooned in the sky like outcasts.

William started to lose height, making big serpentine turns, looking for suitable ground. The squall had passed, the wind had dropped, and the evening was all damp and still in its fickle April manner, sorry for its outburst. Christina's teeth were chattering with cold. She looked down, but Will had dropped into one of his tight corkscrew descents, and she could not bear it. All her insides corkscrewed in sympathy, and she shut her lips tight, ground her teeth, and hid her face in her hands. Will did not need her help in looking. He could do his own looking. She braced herself, remembering Sandy's words: 'The idea is that you pull out before you hit the ground.'

Amazingly, she felt nothing. A final swoop lifted her stomach, but gently, and then the soft bounce of the impact and a smooth, short run to a standstill. The undercarriage sighed, and there was silence, save for the sound of dripping water. She opened her eyes.

'It's not Hendon,' Will was saying. 'But I'm not complaining.'

There were no welcoming crowds waiting to offer help in the damp, empty landscape that stretched out all round them. The only building in sight was a dilapidated barn. There was no friendly farm, no light to be seen, not even a road or a lane. Just sodden pasture, and over a hedge some cows regarding them without interest. Christina stepped down, and felt her shoes fill with mud.

'Ugh!'

'I thought you were a country girl,' Will said.

'I want a hotel,' Christina said.

'There it is,' Will said, pointing to the barn. He looked at her, half laughing, half remorseful.

'They don't seem to have got our booking,' Christina said. 'There's nobody there.'

'They've got a rotten receptionist then, like that "Bunch of

Grapes" place in Kingston.' It was raining again, soft and persistent, without wind. 'Come on,' Will said. 'It's that or nothing. I can't leave the machine. That's my fifty pounds, if anything happens to it.'

'You mean, we've got to sleep there?'

'I've got to. But if you want to look for something better, I'll see if I can find a road or a track or something.'

Christina followed Will over to the barn, her feelings a muddle of outrage and utter weariness. She had no strength to argue. She squelched after Will through mud up to her ankles and into the dark doorway. The barn was full of hay, and warm, and scuttering with tiny life, a pigeon in the rafters, and mice running. The smell of it was Flambards, going through her with the strange pang she had not yet learnt to overcome.

'It smells like home,' she whispered.

'Well, it is, tonight. It couldn't be cosier. Make yourself comfortable. I'll just go and see to the machine, then I'll be back.'

'Kiss it goodnight,' she said.

'Of course.'

Christina did not know whether to laugh or cry. 'Make yourself comfortable!' She sniffed, tremulously. But the hay was warm and sweet. She picked up a handful the way Fowler, the head groom, used to, and smelt it, and crunched it in her fingers. 'Good hard stuff,' she said, as he used to say. She pulled off the wet scarves, listening to all the little movements. She was not afraid of mice, being brought up with stables. She sat in the hay and felt very tired, as if she had come home from a hard day's hunting. It was the same: the mud, the drops of moisture trickling down the back of her neck, the physical exhaustion crushing all emotion save the gorgeous relief of being able to relax. And with it all the extra bliss, the bonus that was unique in her experience and nothing to do with hunting at all—the feeling for Will. 'And he loves me, he wrote it down,' she thought. And he had never known how scared she was; she had come through without letting him down, and he loved her. She slept, as if the barn were paradise. Once she awoke, and heard Will's breathing in the hay somewhere above her. A little vision of Aunt Grace and Mrs. Carter passed through her brain, but she could smile now. Their opinions were thinner, dustier than the very air she breathed.

The final awakening was abrupt, and anything but tender.

'Christina, for heaven's sake, quickly! There are cows everywhere!'

Will was pulling her up bodily from her nest of hay.

'Here, take a stick! We must get out of this place before they wreck the machine!'   —

It was just dawn, bitterly cold, with a drizzle of rain falling. Christina came awake when her feet sank into the mud once more, and a red-eyed animal stood before her, weaving its head uncertainly. Will gave it a resounding wallop over the horns with a pitchfork he had picked up, and it bellowed but did not move. Beyond it in the murk were several others, tails in the air. One had its back to the Blériot and was scratching its hind quarters on the edge of the wing. Another was chewing a bit of fabric on the fuselage. Will lunged forward, dragging Christina with him.

'They're bulls, you fool!' Christina cried out, shattered by her awakening.

Will lashed out at the two offenders, left and right, not caring about their sex. They drew back and stood staring, weaving their heads and stamping their forelegs.

'Get up, Christina, quickly! You know what to do? When I swing the propeller—?'

He was bundling her into the passenger seat, and swinging out with the pitchfork at the same time. The bullocks stood in a menacing semi-circle, lowing impatiently. 'When the engine starts, you've got to switch on and off—that's the switch, there. To give me time to get into my seat, else she'll go off without me. As soon as she surges forward, switch off—then on again. Get away, you blasted brute!'

Christina leaned over into the forward cockpit, groping for the vital switch. She felt dizzy, plunged from deep sleep straight into this drama. She saw Will's tense face as he put his arm up to swing the propeller blade, and the bullocks cavorting on either side, puzzled and dangerous. She could not even remember for a

minute or two how she came to be where she was. She reached for the switch. 'What—?' She had no idea what she was doing. The engine roared, and she felt the machine lurch and quicken beneath her. Will dived beneath the wing and the Blériot moved away with a bound. Christina, desperate not to do the wrong thing, switched off and on, muttering prayers into the cold drops of the morning air, sick with fear and sleep, the thick smells of bullocks and mud and trampled grass in her nostrils. Will took a flying leap into his cockpit and as the machine bounded forward again, Christina gratefully surrendered responsibility, slumping back in her seat. She saw the bullocks galloping and the mud spraying up, the grass blasted flat by the roar of the engine. The cold speared her, slashing her warm face, splintering her hay-barn dreams.

'Will, oh, Will!'

She wanted to cry out, and sob, and protest, shocked awake into this uncomfortable morning. But instead she wound the scarves more firmly round her neck, and blew her nose. The sky lurched in her stomach, and the Blériot climbed. Christina reached for her maps.

CHAPTER 9

Of the fifty pounds William received for delivering the new
Blériot, he sent twenty-five pounds as a first instalment to the
Herr Doktor, repaid five pounds of his debt to Sandy, and spent
the remaining twenty on buying the timber to start building his
new machine. This last purchase was the foundation stone of all
his future ambitions. Everything he did now, Christina knew, was
directed to only one end: the vindication of his aeronautical ideas
in the shape of the 'Dermot'. He instructed for Mr. Adams all
day, for his bread-and-butter money, and worked on the Dermot
all the rest of the time, apart from when he was asleep. Christina
guessed that he slept with the utmost reluctance, but like a log,
after his day's exertions. At week-ends, or whenever the opportunity arose, he gave flips in *Emma* to earn extra money, or com-
peted in any race at Hendon or Brooklands, or Elm Park itself,
which he thought he stood a chance of winning, for the sake of the
prize. Making money this way was something of a gamble, for
the outlay in fuel and making good the inevitable wear and tear
could be for several weeks more than any prize money. Mr.
Adams encouraged him in this flying, for it was a good advertisement for the school, but he was too mean to pay the extra ex-
penses, thinking that he was already generous in allowing Will
the time away.

By the time summer had come, Will's routine seemed to
Christina more or less fixed, with herself merely being useful in the
background whenever she had time off, holding a piece of wood
in place while Will screwed, fetching him a cup of tea from the
café, reassuring a hysterical wife whose husband had been rash
enough to pay for a flight when Will was in one of his playful
moods, or merely waiting, sometimes for hours, for ten minutes

of conversation between pupils. There were no spins in Sandy's car and walks by silent pools in the woods, no rowing in a skiff on the summer Thames as she had once envisaged, no visits to the picture palace or the Kingston Empire. Sandy and Dorothy would do all these things whenever Sandy had time off, and Christina could not help envying them at times, yet she knew she was being irrational. She knew that what Will was doing now was going to decide their whole future together, and—in spite of Will's oblivion of the conventions of courtship—Christina felt secure now in the knowledge that Will did intend to marry her one day. She had no ring, for there was no money to buy one, but to strangers Will introduced Christina as his 'fiancée'. Christina felt she needed this acknowledgement of the situation between them, for at times she could not help wondering just how much Will really needed her. To her, he was her whole world, the only person, her reason for living; to him, sometimes, she thought she was just someone to hold the screws and pass the hammer.

And yet in this strange relationship there was something secure, by its very nature. Sandy would never win Dorothy by such means, Christina thought. Sandy had to work hard for Dorothy, and it showed in his manner at times. 'He's far too good for her. I don't know why he bothers,' Will said shortly, and Christina saw Dorothy's joy in her conquests, the swooping of her long red eyelashes, the innocent, practised invitation in her wide, golden brown eyes. All the boys asked Dorothy out and, although she went more often with Sandy than with anyone else, she went with the others. She was always boating, or going 'up West', or time-keeping at Brooklands, or going to parties. She laughed at Christina, refusing to go with these carefree gangs when she was invited. 'If you come a few times, Bill will pull his socks up, believe me! It's what he needs, darling. You've no idea how to handle the male sex, Christina. You could have an absolutely ripping time if you wanted.'

But Christina did not want a ripping time, not without Will. And the idea of trying to make him jealous was to her pitiful and childish. Whatever might be lacking in their courtship by conventional standards, there was honesty in it, a quality that Dorothy knew nothing of. Christina knew she did not have to bat her eyelashes for Will, or show her legs when she climbed out of the motor-car. He was far more likely to kiss her when a particularly tricky piece of fuselage construction was completed to his satisfaction, than when she leaned against the work-bench showing off her figure.

'Ah, my little beauty,' he would say—not to Christina, but to the skeletal machine propped on trestles in the shed—and he would stroke the smooth spruce, and step back, his eyes shining with aeronautical bliss.

'She's my honey,' he would say, and he would hold out a hand to Christina, and pull her close and give her a hug, so that she dropped the tin of screws she was about to put away in the toolbox.

'Were you talking to me?' Christina murmured one afternoon.

'No, of course I wasn't, slave-girl. I was talking to my own beloved.' His arms went round her, and she felt the wiry hardness of his body, and the fur of sawdust on his cheek.

'Why should I talk to you that way, slave-girl? What have you done to deserve it?'

'Slaved.'

'Oh—' —softly— 'what would I do without you, Christina?'

'Employ a mechanic.'

He kissed her, stopping her jokes, and she knew that none of Dorothy's punting and motoring and partying was worth one minute of the long afternoons in the hangar, and the smell of freshly sawn spruce, and the look in Will's nearly black eyes.

Later, when they went for a cup of tea, Sandy joined them. Will, having had the afternoon off, had pupils to instruct until it was dark, and was waiting for the first one, but Sandy could relax, having been at it all day.

'Have you got next Wednesday afternoon off?' he asked Christina.

'Yes.'

'Adams says I've got to take the Blériot down to some place in Hampshire. There's some old madman down there wants a flight in an aeroplane before he drops dead, and Adams says I'm to go and humour him. What I thought—how about you two coming in *Emma* and we'll have a day out? Picnic and all that, if it's a nice day. The job will only take ten minutes. I know a nice field we can use, flat as a pancake, and there's a wood and a stream and all that. I reckon you could do with being turned out to grass, Will. And I'm darned sure I'm going to make the most of my day out.'

'It's a lovely idea!' Christina said. The flight would be short and harmless, and the idea of a picnic and having nothing to do, and lying in the sunshine and laughing and talking with no pupils to interrupt appealed to her enormously.

'Yes, we could,' Will said. His mind was not where Christina's was, following a different part of Sandy's conversation. 'I wonder what the old maniac, as you call him, is going to pay for this flight?'

'Why?'

'Well—it must be quite a whack, for Adams to think it worthwhile. I was just thinking—that's where you can make money flying, all this private stuff, giving little exhibitions and flying over the holiday resorts, a bit of diving and banking low over the sands—the corporations will pay you quite well for that. And getting in with the rich maniacs, who want to be flown around the countryside. We could do better than working for old Adams.'

'Granted. I'm just too darned lazy to think out anything for myself,' Sandy said.

'Instructing is really making money the hard way.' Will reached for his coat with a groan, as his pupil appeared on a motor-bike at the gates of the field. He pushed back his chair and smiled at Christina. 'Till next Wednesday then, sweetheart. Don't say I don't ever take you out.'

'No, it's very sweet of you to think of it,' Christina said.

Sandy laughed. 'If you're using the Farman,' he called after Will, 'the tension wires want adjusting. She keeps putting her left wing up.' He turned to Christina. 'I'll run you back into Kingston, if you like. I want to see Dorothy, to see if she can come on Wednesday. All right?'

'Oh, yes.' Christina was content.

· · ·

Much to Sandy's annoyance, Dorothy had arranged to go to Brighton with Freddie the following Wednesday, so that when the two machines landed in the field he had earmarked, there were only three of them to share the picnic. Christina, being honest with herself, was pleased that Dorothy wasn't one of the party, for she often found Dorothy's company trying, especially if she was in a mood for provoking the vulnerable Sandy, which she seemed to enjoy. Certainly she had provoked him by going off with Freddie, but by the time Sandy had sampled some of the contents of the picnic bag which Christina had begged from the hotel kitchen, he was in a much more amiable frame of mind.

It was no day for regrets, the sun shining out of a cloudless sky. Sandy's field was heavy with the engine-noise of bees cruising over the powdery-centred buttercups. The promised stream ran slowly through beds of water-flags, then opened out over a shingle bank where the minnows darted like splinters of glass catching the sun. Some old bat willows made deep pools of shade. The crushed grass beneath the picnic rug smelled of stream-beds and summer. Christina lay listening to the whine of midges and the distant double-calling of a cuckoo in the woods, the whirring of a hay reaper two fields away and the occasional shout of the farm-boy to his horses. Noisy, she thought, with a blissful sigh at the peacefulness of such noise. The sun was warm through the thinness of her blouse. It was like the few moments on the beach at Hardelot, but sweeter this time, because there were no fears. 'This is how it should be, always,' she thought, and the past fears and the future fears were all lost in the sound of bees and the cuckoo, in Will's laugh, in Sandy's lazy rejoinder, the reaper's soft click-clacking. She turned her head, squinting into the sun, and watched Will, in a white shirt and his flying breeches, lying propped on his elbows eating a veal pie. He was talking shop, but Christina did not care. Pégoud . . . she caught the name. It was the name of a Frenchman who had turned a plane over on its back so that it had made a somersault in the air. They had been talking about nothing else since it had happened.

'You remember what I said about those fish, eh?' Will said to her. 'Who said it was impossible?'

'Me, of course,' Christina said, humouring him.

'The old boy wanted me to do it,' Sandy said. 'He'd read it in the newspapers. "Loop the loop, young fellow," he bawled in my ear. No straps or anything. I told you he was a maniac. I told him the wings would fall off, so he didn't press me any more.'

'How much did he pay you?' Will asked.

'Twenty pounds.'

'There. For nothing! And old Adams sitting at home collecting twenty pounds while you do all the work. We really must get organized, Sandy. I bet if we could do loops we could really make some money. It'll be all the rage for a bit—after all, if they flock to the flying-field at the week-ends just to see a few races round pylons, and a bit of trick flying—spirals and banking—what will they do if someone offers to loop the loop for them? They'd come in their droves.'

'Mmm.' Sandy sounded less enthusiastic. 'Yes, I imagine the promoters will push it.' He paused, selecting a tomato. 'Why? Would you fancy making money that way?'

'I fancy making money, that's all,' Will said gloomily. 'I still owe the doctor two hundred pounds, apart from all I want for the machine.'

'You'd want a good manager, and a good aeroplane,' Sandy said. 'That's all.'

'I've got a good aeroplane.'

'Adams would be a good manager, if you handled him right. If you showed him you could do it, I bet he'd do all the donkey-work. If he thought there was money in it he would, anyway.'

Will rolled over on to his back and lay gazing into the sky. Christina watched him, her pleasure quenched by the direction the talk had taken. He was silent for a long time. Christina started picking blades of grass, frowning. Sandy reached for a bottle of ginger beer and sat up, drinking contentedly.

'Want some?' he said to Will.

'*Emma* would do it, you know,' Will said, not hearing him.

Sandy was silent.

'She's stronger than a Blériot, and Pégoud did it in a standard Blériot. He only set the wires at a bigger angle from the cabane.'

'He put a bigger tail on.'

'*Emma*'s tail's all right as it is.'

'All right. She'd do it,' Sandy agreed in his amiable way.

'Yes.' Will sat up. His expression was absent, calculating. He drank the ginger beer Sandy passed him, and took another tomato. not saying anything. Christina lay on her stomach picking more blades of grass, miserable with these new thoughts. Miserable, more, that they had come to disturb this paradise: in the oily gloom of the old shed they would not have been out of place.

'The biggest strain would come at the bottom of the dive, before you go over. I can't see that there's anything else. She'd take that, I'm sure. I'm going to try it.'

Sandy's head jerked up. 'What, now?'

'Yes. No time like the present.' Will had stood up, and was smiling, his body taut and excited. 'Why?' he said to Sandy. 'There's nothing wrong?'

Sandy shrugged. 'No. What about straps?'

'There'll be a piece of rope we can use over in the farmyard. I'll go and see. It won't take a minute.'

He turned and started hurrying away across the grass, jog-trotting in his eagerness. Christina went on lying there, staring after him, her chin resting on her hands. He had not for one moment given her a thought in this train of events, and she was expected to venture no opinion. She was expected to go on en-joying her picnic, while he gambled with his life over her head. With quivering self-control, she went on lying there, blindly pulling at the grass.

'Is he mad?' she said to Sandy, her voice shaking.

Sandy looked at her kindly. 'Impetuous, shall we say?'

Christina let out a little moan, and clenched her hands.

'Come on, Christina. Look as if you're loving it,' Sandy said wryly. 'There's nothing else you can do, you know.'

'What, when the wings fall off?'

'They won't fall off.'

'How do you know?'

'Will was working out his stresses, sitting there with his ginger beer. And his mathematics have never failed him yet.'

'So much for our day out!' Christina stood up abruptly, feeling she could happily have kicked all the picnic things into the stream. 'So much for your day doing nothing!'

'Come on, girl. You know your Will by now, surely? You wouldn't change him for a stockbroker, would you? Or that horsy brother of his?'

It was true, after all. She had known. Will himself had told her he would make her unhappy 'because of flying', and she had laughed then when he had told her she would be afraid. She hadn't known then what fear was.

She pushed her hair back with her hands, saying no more. Will was coming back, trailing great loops of rope, and they went across the grass to meet him. Christina composed her face. She helped turn *Emma* round, and held out Will's coat for him.

'Is there anything loose in the cockpit?' Sandy said.

Between them they removed a tool-kit and some maps and a pair of gloves, while Will checked over the machine. Will was quiet now, and Sandy had no more jokes. Christina, looking at Will, saw that he was nervous, but appreciated that this was scarcely to be wondered at. It just made her more angry, that he had to make himself suffer, as well as the rest of them, when they could still be lying in the warm grass drinking ginger beer.

Sandy anchored one end of the rope underneath the cockpit seat and Will got in and settled himself. Sandy brought the rope up between Will's legs and over his shoulder and down again under the seat and up over the other shoulder, pulling it tight, while Christina looked on, picturing the machine crashing and setting on fire, and Will all trussed up and unable to get out. She had no doubt that the thought was not entirely absent from his own mind, but nobody said anything. The sun was still shining, and the reaper going two fields away, and Christina noticed that the hem of her skirt was all yellow with pollen.

Sandy finished off with a large reef-knot round Will's waist. 'Fall out of that if you can,' he remarked, and slid down. 'All set?'

Will nodded. Sandy went round to swing the propeller, and Will switched on. He did not glance at Christina, but she could have given him no encouragement, standing there trying to be glad that he was not a stockbroker, biting her lips to stop them trembling. 'A picnic!' she was thinking bitterly. 'A *picnic* . . .'

Will took *Emma* down the field and turned her at the bottom in order to take off into the wind. Sandy and Christina walked back out of the way in silence, and turned as the little machine started her take-off. The field was much rougher than the aerodrome, and she bounced alarmingly once or twice, but by the time she had reached their end again she was off the ground and climbing, the sun sparking off her wires. For all Will's mathematics she looked to Christina as frail as a dragonfly as she skimmed over the old farm buildings.

Sandy flung himself down in the grass and lay with his hands behind his head, his eyes half-shut against the sunlight.

'Relax, Christina. It'll take him several minutes to make enough height. I don't think he'll try it much below four thousand.'

Christina sat down, arranged her skirt, and waited. For all Sandy's attitude she did not think he was any more relaxed than she was, squinting at the laboriously climbing insect impaled on the blue sky. The reaper had stopped, no doubt to watch the unfamiliar sight, but the cuckoo still called, over and over. The more height Will gained, the safer his antics would be, giving him room to gain control should anything go wrong, and Christina wanted to spin the minutes out, painful as they were. She picked a few buttercups, threading their stalks to make a chain, and Sandy watched her, not saying anything. The noise of *Emma*'s engine grew fainter and fainter, and the cuckoo sang very close, covering it up. Sandy glanced at his watch.

'I should think he'd be happy enough with that,' he remarked.

The aircraft was now very high to Christina's eyes, but perfectly plain to see. She stood up, shading her eyes against the sun. Sandy got to his feet too. Christina could hear her heart beating high up in her throat, constricting her breathing, and she tried to comfort herself: 'It will be over in a minute. It can't last long, this awful feeling.'

And as she watched, *Emma*'s nose dipped and she started to dive down. Gradual at first, the dive steepened. Christina clenched her hands.

'Here we go,' Sandy murmured. 'Yow! That's a boy!'

Emma was vertical, screaming like an angry mosquito in the shimmering blue. Christina shuddered as she pulled out, shutting her eyes for a moment, thinking of the strain on the wings, but the little machine reared up, whole and eager, flashing like a diamond,

still very high. Christina could scarcely make out what had happened. The nose of the machine was pointing up, vertical, and then she seemed to stop, and hang, in an utter silence, like a bird shot in full-flight.

'*Sandy*!' Christina was petrified.

Then *Emma* started to fall like a stone, still in a vertical position but tail-first. Christina could hear the machine whining, the sun still picking it out so that it was almost impossible to look. She felt great wracks of hysterical fear seize her throat; she turned to Sandy in agony.

'What—?'

'Tail-sliding,' Sandy said laconically. He reached out an arm and put it round her shoulders, not taking his eyes off *Emma*.

'Is it—?'

'He'll get her out. You watch.' He gave Christina a comforting shake, so that she was able to look again. *Emma* was still plummeting down on her tail but as Christina watched she saw the machine swing like a pendulum and drop her nose with a wrench that seemed to bring her up all standing. Sandy's hand clenched for a moment on Christina's shoulder.

The next moment *Emma* was diving nose-first, gradually pulling out into normal flight.

Sandy let Christina go, and scratched his nose thoughtfully. 'He doesn't want to make a habit of that,' he said. He looked at Christina, and grinned. 'I bet that made him feel sick!'

'Oh!' Christina was speechless now with what felt like rage more than anything else. It was not over. *Emma* was climbing once more. It was all going to happen again, and she must wait, and pick buttercups, while *Emma* gained height again. She was choked with bitterness, and could not answer Sandy's apparent amusement. She turned away, kicking the grass, listening to *Emma*'s high, distant labour, until it should cease, and turn into a whine again. The foolishness of it appalled her—that it *mattered* . . . What good was it? What sort of strain had *Emma* taken coming out of the tail-dive, that Sandy's fingers had tightened like that? Sandy was giving nothing away now, chewing a piece of grass, waiting and watching.

'Here she comes,' he said.

Christina watched again, cold and angry. *Emma* was diving almost beyond the vertical. Her engine roared as she came out of the bottom and went into the steep, zooming climb. Up . . . up . . . Christina winced, bit her lip and felt the blood on her tongue. She saw the farmyard rope holding Will, cutting his shoulders . . . *Emma*'s engine cut out, but her nose was over the top. She seemed to lurch, spreadeagled, then fall away off the top, sliding out sideways, screaming again as if she could not stand such ill-treatment. Down, down, her tail over the vertical. Christina felt sick, seeing Will trussed there, the wind shrieking past him and all the world on the top of his head. How did you know what was push and pull when you were like that, and up and down? And the difference between push and pull was being alive and being dead.

'Oh!' she spat out angrily, shaking back her hair.

'He's done it,' Sandy said. He smiled at Christina. 'And the wings didn't drop off.'

Emma was diving under control now, the right way up, tidy and normal. Christina was drained and tired, with none of the exhilaration and excitement she knew she ought to feel. She smiled bleakly at Sandy, and he gave her a little fatherly pat, and said, 'He's a boy, your Will. Quite a display! Very nice. He'll be feeling very pleased with himself.'

He was. They ran to meet him, and disentangle him from the ropes. He was as white as a sheet—'Oh, that veal pie!' he murmured—but then the talk was all of fuel supply and rudder control and wing stresses, and Christina left them poring over the petrol tank, discussing an adjustment to the vent, and walked away across the grass back to the picnic debris. She started to gather the things together, swatting at the midges, screwing the paper up and pushing it into the hold-all with the remains of the pie and the squashed tomatoes.

She heard the reaper resume its work over its fields. She was hot again now. She walked over to the shingle bank, and lay down, trailing her hands in the water. The minnows sprang away at her first shadow, and the water ran on alone, cool and thin. Christina laid her cheek on her arm and started to cry, not meaning to, but unable to stop. It was a lament for the brief hour of the picnic, that had got lost and been frightened away, like the shoal of flashing minnows.

CHAPTER 10

Will spent two weeks strengthening *Emma*'s wings and improving the power of her controls, and then practised looping over Elm Park. Not only Mr. Adams, but everyone on the airfield, was impressed, and turned out to watch the displays. Will then strengthened the Blériot so that he could loop that too. And Sandy said he was losing his reputation, and did his first loop in the Blériot. Although everyone on the field understood how the manoeuvre was performed, and although all agreed there was nothing dangerous about it in a suitable aircraft, nobody else at Elm Park followed suit.

'In another year, when aircraft are stronger and better powered, everyone will be doing it,' Will said. 'If we want to earn some money at it, now is the time to put it to Adams.'

It was a year since he had had the operation performed on his knee, and he had paid under a third of what he owed. This debt was anathema to his scrupulous nature, and when Christina protested about his plans for earning money he was short with her. She said no more. She knew better. She knew that within a year he was also going to need several hundred pounds to buy an engine for the Dermot, slowly and painfully taking shape in the shed.

'She is what matters, ultimately,' Will said, almost angry. 'I'm not doing circus tricks for the sake of showing off. I'm doing them purely for money. It's debasing flying, if you like, turning it into a circus, I won't argue with that. But I'd be a fool not to take this opportunity to get money.'

'What do the crowds come to see?' Christina said in a low voice. 'In their hearts they want to see a crash.'

Will did not reply. A week later, when Christina went to Elm Park on her afternoon off, she arrived to find the fire tender out on the field, and the crumpled, smoking carcass of a Morane-Saulnier blotting the smooth grass, one tattered wing sticking up into the sky. Groups of people stood silently about, watching. Something was being lifted into an ambulance. Christina saw Will holding the ambulance door, and Sandy standing beside him with his hands in his pockets. The ambulance drove away, and the bystanders started to drift apart. Will and Sandy came back together. They both looked white and stricken, and Will had blood all over his trousers.

'Who—who was it?' Christina asked.

'That little fellow—Claud something-or-other—he drives a blue Renault. Drove a blue Renault, I should say.' Sandy wiped a hand wearily across his forehead. 'He won't drive anything any more.'

'He should have learned to drive an aeroplane,' Will said. 'Before trying to show off to his girl-friend.'

'His girl-friend?'

'Yes, she was watching. They took her into the café.'

Will went to change into some clean trousers, and Christina stood watching the crash team clearing up the mess out on the field. The girl in the café, she thought, could well have been herself. She had struggled, God only knew, to stop being afraid of this flying thing, but every time she made a little progress, and accepted as normal something that had frightened her earlier, so Will went on to something new. Now it was loops and bunts, soon it would be testing the Dermot, later . . . who could tell? Already she had heard it suggested that it was not ridiculous any more to consider flying the Atlantic. 'So it's no good thinking there won't be anything worse to come,' she thought. 'It won't improve.' It merely meant that *she* must improve. Grow up, or grow hard—she did not know which. Or merely keep on covering it up, not saying anything. The only thing that made Will angry was when she showed that she was afraid.

Sandy came up and gave her nose a friendly tweak. 'Cheer up, gel, it wasn't your boy-friend. Your boy-friend doesn't believe in girls standing idly around watching the men do all the work. Your boy-friend wants you to do some riveting this afternoon. He told me so. So look all keen and eager. Start smiling.'

She smiled. But even Will could not cover up his feelings this time, and they spent a miserable afternoon working. A subdued air hung over the airfield. There was no banter, or whistling, and a knot of morbid sightseers gathered at the gate to watch the wreck being cleared up.

A fortnight later a promoter from Hendon watched Will put *Emma* through her tricks and signed him up to give an exhibition the following Sunday. Adams had agreed to act as an agent and get Will all the exhibition work he could, for a cut of ten per cent, and Will agreed to go on instructing whenever he was free. It was a start. He was full of optimism.

'Twenty pounds! Two for Adams—well, I can afford that. Eighteen pounds for ten minutes' work! I call that handsome.'

Even Christina had to agree. She went to Hendon with Dorothy, joining the great throng in the enclosure, holding on to the new hat she had bought for the occasion. 'If Bill's going to be famous, darling, you've got to be a credit to him,' Dorothy had told her. She had known that the Hendon meetings were well-patronized, but this gay crowd of some fifty thousand enthusiasts with its picnic hampers and lines of motor-cars astonished her. Its enthusiasm was infectious. She found herself getting excited over the races, and cheering and waving her programme with the best of them, but when it was time for Will to do his piece, she found she was shaking with nerves, almost as if she was going to do it herself. She knew he had practised day in and day out so that the loops were now perfect circles, and the high screaming bunt which she hated so much a smoothly drawn figure of compass-like precision, but when *Emma* took off and started to gain height, she was as sick with fear as she had been the very first day with the cuckoo calling in the hot Hampshire field. Dorothy glanced at her white face, and gave her hand a friendly squeeze. The great crowd, which before had been shouting with excitement with a noise like a rough sea breaking over shingle, was now settling into an uneasy hush, everyone straining their faces up towards the clear sky where little *Emma* laboured. Christina knew that Will would sacrifice height in order not to bore the crowd; she had heard him discussing the subject with Sandy. *Emma* was not an exceptional climber, and Will had worked out that three minutes' peering up at the sky was enough to give a spectator a stiff neck. Even his showmanship was subject to mathematics. So that when he started his dive, Christina was not at all surprised to see that he was a good deal lower than he had been on the first occasion.

Clasping her hat with icy fingers she watched *Emma*'s dive turn beyond the vertical into the inverted leg of the bunt, the long backward curve of the vertical S that he was tracing in the sky. The crowd was quite still and silent, and only *Emma* was screaming, as if in protest at the unnatural evolution she was performing, head over heels in the autumn sun. Then she dropped into the vertical again, and pulled out, smooth and fast, whistling over the airfield past the stands, and the crowd gave a great sigh all in unison, in perfect accord, like the sound of a gust of wind in the trees. Satisfaction—or disappointment? Christina felt herself shaking with the awful rage she had found before, a great mixture of scorn for her own feebleness and resentment at the greed of this muttering crowd, preying on the antics of a frail monoplane. 'Oh, you fool!' she whispered to herself. 'You fool!' But she could not change it.

After the bunt Will climbed again and did four loops one after the other, then he landed, and was asked to take up several members of the public to perform a loop—one at a time—which he did. Christina could not get near him for the great press of the crowd.

'He's a great success!' Dorothy was full of excitement. 'Oh, Christina, just think, they're bound to ask him again, and he'll be rich in no time! You'll be able to get married!'

'Married! But he's not twenty yet!'

'Why, what difference does that make?'

But Christina, in the hour of Will's triumph, was not going to tell Dorothy that Will was not old enough yet to discard his father's authority.

She drove back to Elm Park with Dorothy, weary with all her conflicting emotions, and arrived almost at the same time as Will and Sandy in *Emma* and the Blériot respectively. Sandy had won a race and ten pounds, and Will had been asked to fly again on four more Sundays, so everyone was in high spirits. The two girls went out on to the field to meet them. It was a warm autumn evening with a big glowing sun disappearing in a haze of smoky gold behind the yellowing birch-trees.

'We ought to celebrate!' Dorothy laughed. 'Take us up and give us a loop! I've never done it yet! I want to have something to boast about—'

'Yes, of course—that's a splendid idea!' Sandy said, taking her arm. 'I'll take you. Will's tired, poor boy. I'll loop you silly.'

Will was laughing. 'I'll take Christina! We'll all do it—a celebration loop.'

'Before the sun goes!' Dorothy was already running across to the Blériot, stumbling in her tight skirt, laughing with excitement. Will grabbed Christina's hand and ran with her too.

'Will!'

'What's the matter? Oh, your silly skirt—' Close beside *Emma*, he turned and lifted her up bodily, putting her into the passenger's cockpit.

'This is two guineas' worth, all for nothing. Aren't you lucky?' he laughed. He bent over and kissed her, groping for the straps at the same time. 'You'll look lovely flying in that hat. Here, tie it on with my scarf.'

He pulled off his scarf and tied it over her hat and under her chin, turning the wide brim up at the front, and pulling it well down at the back. Christina didn't know whether to laugh or cry. 'Please, Will, I don't—'

'Don't what? Love me? Nonsense. Of course you love me. Twice as much upside-down.'

He was in a crazy mood, all the work and practising of the past few weeks vindicated by the day's success. Christina felt breathless, wanting to protest, but not able to find the words. He was fastening the straps over her shoulders, pulling them tight, so that she was imprisoned in her seat, powerless to move. She heard Dorothy laughing again. The sun was in her eyes, flaming down the field in its last dying gesture, reddening the whole sky so that the dusk behind them was all amber and smoke, dark and light at the same time.

'What a sky to fly in!' Will said, and the next moment the two machines were moving off down the grass side by side. They bumped across the field, then Will was gesturing to Sandy to go ahead. Christina saw Dorothy's hair streaming out like a red banner as the Blériot gathered speed. She thought, 'This is crazy. This can't be going to happen . . .' But then it was *Emma* racing over the grass, as if she would charge the red tip of the sinking sun. 'Oh, no, I can't do it,' Christina thought.

As *Emma* climbed, Christina grew colder and colder, both physically and mentally. She watched the sun grow from an edge over the trees into a round, glowing ball again; she saw Sandy climbing above them and thought she could still see Dorothy's mane, and hear her laugh. Her own hair was flying out now. Without goggles her eyes were smarting, the straps were cutting into her shoulders. She did not want to loop the loop. 'I can't,' she kept thinking, as *Emma* climbed. 'I can't do it.'

She tapped Will on the shoulder. He half-turned his head, smiling.

'I don't want to!' she yelled. 'Don't do it!'

He did not hear her. He smiled again, cheerfully. She shook her head, but he had turned away, and was looking up at Sandy some fifty feet above them.

Christina began to feel desperate. She looked down, and quite suddenly, as if it was there again, never having been removed by the crash tender, she saw the smoking debris of the Morane-Saulnier, and the blood all over Will's clothes. She saw *Emma* doing the bunt, and never straightening out, falling and falling until she hit the ground in a great whoosh of dust and flame. She started to struggle against the straps, trying to reach forward to tell Will.

'I don't want to!' she screamed.

Will turned his head and shouted something. It sounded like, 'You'll love it,' but Christina could no longer control herself. 'I won't!' she screamed at him. 'I won't do it.'

She reached up and pulled the straps off over her shoulders. Then she leaned forward, half-standing in the cockpit, and put her head close to Will's. He had no helmet on, only goggles, his hair flattened by the wind.

'Don't do it!' she shouted in his ear, her hair tearing loose in a wild streaming cloud round her face. 'Don't do it!'

This time his head jerked round as far as his own straps would allow, his eyes wide with amazement. He shouted something, roughly—she could not tell what—and jabbed over his shoulder with his thumb.

'I won't!' she shouted in his ear. 'I won't do it.'

He turned back, and put the nose of the machine down suddenly. Christina held on to the front of the cockpit, for one terrible moment thinking that Will in some fit of madness was going ahead with his plans, angry enough to fling her out and kill her. But the dive was not steep enough to dislodge her, only steep enough to set the wind screaming and shrieking through her hair, knifing through her body, setting her teeth on edge. Round *Emma* went in big, angry spirals, protesting wildly, swooping and twisting, Christina's stomach heeling and retching all the way. Blinded by hair, her eyes streaming in the icy wind, she felt rather than saw *Emma* touch, and run bouncing over the grass. She was ashamed and horrified by what she had done, but knew she would do it again if forced to it. She could not help herself.

Will was furious, as she had guessed he would be.

He got down, pulled off his goggles and looked at her with an expression of cold contempt.

'What did you want to do? Kill yourself? Are you mad?'

She did not reply.

She climbed down slowly, holding on to the wing. She was trembling with cold, clenching her teeth to keep them from chattering. Her hair was in a great tangle down her back, her lovely new hat flown away, tears from her smarting eyes smearing her cheeks. But she wasn't crying; in spite of everything, she wasn't going to give in completely. She pushed her hair back, and pulled off the scarf which was still tied under her chin.

'Here's your scarf.'

Will snatched it from her without a word and turned and walked off towards his shed. Christina knew he would not look back. She turned too, and walked towards the car-park to wait for Dorothy, her logic all blotted out by a seething rage at the injustice meted out to her. No one but an obsessive maniac would treat a girl the way Will had treated her, she thought, cartwheeling her through the sky and expecting her to laugh with joy. He never treated her as though she was precious, as other men treated girls. He treated her like a—like—like an *equal*. And it was this ultimate compliment, and her failure to rise to it, that set the tears flowing. She sat huddled in Dorothy's Ford in the dark car-park, sobbing, the rug pulled over her head.

Driving home, she tried to explain what had happened to Dorothy. She tried to justify herself, telling Dorothy how she had seen the crashed Morane-Saulnier down on the ground, as if it was still in fact there.

'Will ought to understand,' she said softly. 'When he broke his leg, he told me he was so frightened when he saw the jump coming up that he fell off because he fainted with fright. He *told* me that! He wasn't even ashamed.' And the parallel went further, although she did not tell Dorothy this, for Will had seen his own father crushed and almost killed by a falling horse at a similar jump a few years earlier. Perhaps Will had thought of that, at the last moment, as she had seen the Morane-Saulnier.

'Yes, it's too bad of him,' Dorothy said. 'I don't blame you a bit. I was scared out of my wits. I screamed my head off. And Sandy just laughed. I thought he was going to die laughing.'

She changed gear with a jerk, impatient with men's ways, and rabbits' eyes glowed in the light of the lamps, and the coldness of autumn touched the darkness, nipping through their motoring veils. Christina said no more.

CHAPTER 11

In spite of Dorothy's sympathy, Christina was ashamed of herself in a way she had never been before. She could not forget the contempt in Will's face. She slept badly, dozing and dreaming, and thought of the days before she saw Will again as aeons of time in which to suffer this hideous feeling of humiliation. And suppose when she saw him again he looked at her in the same way? She could not bear to think of it.

By the time it was light she had decided to resolve the situation. Monday morning was always slack, and with luck she would not be needed in the office until ten. She dressed and slipped downstairs when only the chambermaids were up, and fetched the old bicycle Dorothy had given her and set off for Elm Park. It was cold and still, the trees across the commons looped with wet cobwebs. Christina had a cold feeling inside her, full of anxiety and this awful shame. She put her head down and pedalled fast, her thick skirt billowing round her ankles.

So concerned with her tangled feelings, she had never given a thought to the effect her arrival at this hour of the morning would have on Will, and did not realize what sort of a ménage she would disturb with her headlong intrusion. As she pushed open the small door set into the larger doors of Will's shed, she smelt the sharp, pleasant smell of bacon frying. The electric light was on at the far end; she squeezed round *Emma*'s wing-tip and called out, 'Will!'

Will was shaving, peering into a tiny bit of mirror wedged in a rough bit of the wall. He had nothing on save a towel tied round his middle. Joe, now Mr. Adams' official mechanic, was just pouring water out of the kettle into a teapot, using the partly-built wing of the Dermot, propped on trestles with a piece of tarpaulin over it, as a table. On a small oilstove a frying-pan smoked and sizzled, completing as domestic a scene as any in the kitchen of 'The Bunch of Grapes'. Joe looked up, swinging the hot water over the floor in his surprise, grinning all over his face, while Will turned round in astonishment, the cut-throat razor still to his cheek.

'Morning, Miss Christina,' Joe said. 'Cup of tea?'

Christina's hand went up to her face in a gesture of horror, embarrassment flooding her. Her eyes went to Will and instantly, with as quick a shock of pure, irreverent amusement, she knew that Will could not quench her again with his scorn. How could he be scornful, dressed only in a towel, with lather all over his face? She composed herself more quickly than he did.

'Thank you very much,' she said to Joe. 'I would like one.'

'What on earth—?' Will looked round for a towel, found he was wearing it, and stood helplessly for a moment, glaring at her.

'Cup of tea, Will?' Joe said, diplomatically.

Will turned his scowl on Joe. 'Yes. And find me a towel, for heaven's sake.' He turned his back and went on shaving. 'What on earth possessed you to call at this time of day?' he asked Christina.

'I'm sorry about last night,' Christina said.

'Do you want me to leave you?' Joe said, flipping a tea-towel at Will.

'No, we don't,' Will said irritably. 'Yes, I'm sorry about last night too. What do you intend to do about it?'

'I came to tell you I'm not frightened any more, and if you take me up again I'll prove it to you.'

If Will was surprised, it was impossible to tell. He washed his face and dried himself on the tea-towel, then gathered up his shirt and trousers and went round behind *Emma* to get dressed.

Christina sat wondering if it was wise to have made such an offer: it was like having offered to jump off a cliff into a bottomless ocean merely to get him to smile at her again. She loved him so hopelessly—and he was so thin. Seeing his white ribs sticking out like the frames of a boat made her love him in a terrible tender, maternal way, so that she wanted to cook him meat pies and wash his shirts. Yet she knew she wasn't much of a cook, and he, for all his ribs showing, was as hard as nails. She had no pride, riding on her bicycle at this ungodly hour merely because she could not stand the memory of his angry face. She bent her head down over the hot teacup, burning with a shame worse almost than the shame of being afraid of looping the loop. He had not even been gracious over her offer. He could trample her now like a doormat, and she would deserve it. She was indeed a stupid fool.

'Bit of bacon, Miss Christina?' Joe asked amiably. 'There's plenty.'

She shook her head. Will came back and took the pan off Joe, forking the bacon straight into his mouth.

'We could go up now, if you want to,' he said, very non-committal. 'If that's what you've come for.'

'Yes.'

Christina helped them wheel *Emma* out of the shed into the cold, grey morning. Joe refuelled the machine, and Christina fetched the flying-coat and got wrapped up, and got in, and Will did up the straps for her again. She could not read his expression at all. 'I must be mad to be doing this,' she told herself, and there was no reply to it, no question at all but that she was mad. As *Emma* climbed, and the roofs of Elm Park grew fainter and fainter below, she sat shivering in every nerve. The back of Will's head showed nothing. 'He would have felt like this,' she thought bitterly, 'having his bones broken in Switzerland, if there had been no chloroform.' But there was no blessed chloroform for her.

Suddenly wisps of thick grey mist started streaming past. The ground disappeared. Christina looked round, startled, and saw nothing beyond the wing-tips, only thick, blotted cloud. It came up from below; there was nothing, only this engulfing wet web of blind air.

Emma's nose dropped. Christina saw Will's hand come up and release his own straps, so that he could shrug them off. He switched off the engine, and *Emma* was gliding down, and Will turning round in his seat.

'We can't do it!' he shouted. 'The cloud's too low. It would be dangerous.'

Christina gulped the wet cloud, the dearest cloud in the world. She loved it, thick and secure round the zooming space that Will loved. She pulled off her straps too and leaned forward. 'What a pity!' She could not keep the joy out of her voice.

Will turned round again. He was laughing. 'You liar!' he shouted.

'Yes!' she shouted back deliriously. They were coming out of the cloud now, Elm Park all spread out for inspection, even the dark patch where the Morane-Saulnier had smouldered. She put her head close to Will's ear and shouted, 'I love you!' He turned his head again, and she kissed his cheek, all smooth and smelling of fresh soap, even over the smell of burning oil. 'Seven hundred feet!' he shouted. 'That's beaten Sandy's record for kissing!' And the incident was closed, and never referred to again.

The following morning Dorothy came to her in the office, giggling with some marvellous suppressed amusement.

'Whatever's the matter?' Christina asked, busy with a tricky letter on the typing machine.

'I've had a marvellous idea,' she said. 'For Wednesday afternoon. The boys promised to take us out.'

'Did they?'

'Yes. What with Will's exhibition money and Sandy's race money, it's high time we had an afternoon out—you, especially. Will never takes you anywhere. I decided we should do something *we* would like to do for a change. We're going riding. I've hired four horses.'

Christina stared at her. 'They'll never come!'

'Sandy will,' Dorothy said. 'And how can Will refuse? I've

been to the stables and chosen the horses we'll have. Two-thirty, Wednesday afternoon. We'll leave here as soon as we've had lunch.'

Christina laughed. She would never have dared submit such a programme to Will herself, but was intensely curious as to how he would receive it. She very much doubted whether he would accept the invitation. In the evening, when she was free, she unfolded her riding habit out of her tin trunk and shook it out, and the smell of it, and the shine on the lovely boots and the jauntiness of the hard bowler overwhelmed her with longing for Wednesday afternoon to come. Even if Will wouldn't come, she thought, she must go, just this once, to satisfy this nostalgic desire that Dorothy's words had roused in her.

For once, on Wednesday afternoon, Christina knew she was immaculately dressed. She felt more at home in her riding clothes than in any others she had, and although Dorothy's habit was smart enough, she did not wear it with the same ease. Christina sensed this, and felt marvellous. And it was for Dorothy to handle Will. She was having no part of it.

When Sandy and Will saw them, they looked surprised. Will, in fact, looked stunned.

'I thought we were going out together?' he said.

'We are,' Dorothy said. 'We're going riding.'

'You're joking,' Will said. He looked hard at Christina.

'It's no good blaming Christina, Bill. This is my idea,' Dorothy said firmly. 'Sandy's coming. He promised he would, didn't you?' she darted at him, belligerently.

'So help me, in a weak moment, I did,' Sandy said. 'But I thought you'd forget all about it.'

'Bad luck, then. I didn't. You're coming, because you promised, so that leaves you, Bill. You've absolutely no excuse, I'm afraid.'

'No, I haven't. Only that I'm petrified,' Will said.

'Oh, really!' Dorothy wouldn't stand for this. 'Upside-down at five thousand feet, and yet you're frightened of a tame nag with all four of its legs on the ground! That won't do, Bill. Will it, Christina?'

Christina said nothing. She looked at Will, and found him looking back at her, cornered. She knew then that he would not refuse, because she had offered to loop with him. The thing was complementary. Christina had not meant that he should be manoeuvred like this, and she was sorry for him, but it was fair. He saw the justice of it too, and laughed.

'As long as it's just a boxkite of a horse, then, a 1909 Farman type, good and underpowered. And never again—when I could be working safely in my shed . . .' He shook his head sorrowfully.

But when they arrived at the stables, the two horses led out for the men were sixteen-hand brutes with white-rimmed eyes. The groom held a liver-chestnut that flattened its ears and switched its tail irritably, and looked at Will.

'I think Sultan here will suit you, sir. He's full of go.'

'Oh, no thanks. I'm not riding that! Put the side-saddle on it and let Christina have it. I'll have that grey.'

The groom looked astounded. The two animals saddled with side-saddles were contented looking beasts, the grey actually dozing while it waited, its white eyelashes dropped down like veils.

'I don't think Sultan's a lady's horse, sir—'

'Well, I want a lady's horse,' Will said. 'Christina can ride anything. You don't have to bother about her. You'll ride Sultan, won't you?' He turned to her, half-joking, half in real entreaty.

'Yes, yes, I will,' she said hastily. 'Of course.'

Dorothy's laugh peeled out. 'The way you treat Christina—!'

The groom, looking very disapproving, changed the saddles, and gave Christina a leg up on the restless Sultan.

'He's very strong, miss,' he warned anxiously. But as Christina gathered up her reins, he relaxed, and smiled at her. 'He's a good horse, if you can ride him.'

Christina could feel it already. Her heart warmed to this wonderful feeling of strength and eagerness beneath her. It was beyond all expectations, to have a horse like this. She looked at Will, and laughed with delight. He watched her admiringly, a disturbed light in his eye.

'Why,' he said softly, 'it almost makes me feel as if Mark—' Then he stopped, and made a face at her. 'Hallucinations. It's all too much like the bad old Flambards days, as far as I'm concerned.'

'You can bear it just this once,' Christina said. 'Come on.' She was shaken by his reference to Mark, for she, too, had thought inevitably of Mark. She had scarcely ever ridden without Mark somewhere at hand, on his magnificent bay, Treasure. Sultan was a horse Mark would have liked.

'Just this once,' Will agreed, and mounted the grey.

Christina had never seen Will on a horse, in all her life. She knew—for it was a family fact—that he was the 'worst of all the Russells' when it came to riding, but she realized at once as soon as she saw him that even the worst of all the Russells was still better than most of the common run. After all, he had ridden day in and day out all his life until the age of thirteen. One did not forget. Somehow, the fact that Will could ride, in spite of everything, pleased Christina enormously.

She got the eager Sultan to walk beside Will's mare, but could feel his impatience beneath her as they left the gravel road and turned on to a sandy track. She felt as eager as he did.

'Oh, come on,' she shouted to Will. 'Let's canter!'

'All right. Open the throttle.'

Sultan was away the moment Christina eased the reins, darting ahead of Will's mare. Christina glanced back to see that Will was all right, not wanting to set the others off with her own excitement, but the other horses were unaffected by their impetuous companion, and she had nothing to worry about. They broke into a trot, but Sultan was cantering, and reaching for his head, flicking his tail with impatience.

'Oh, you're lovely!' Christina said to him, and sat down and let him go.

Oh, she had forgotten! The feel of it intoxicated her, the great easy rhythm beneath her and the hard drumming of hooves spitting up sand, the trees leaping past in the cold sunlight. She saw the long, bold ears pricked up, and the red mane streaming, and thought of Treasure and Drummer and Sweetbriar and Wood-pigeon with a fierce twist of longing—all the lovely Flambards horses whose ways and tricks she had learned. She sat still, screwing up her eyes into the wind. The others were left behind, but the wide, soft track curved invitingly through banks of bracken towards a ridge of pine-trees: it was galloping country, and Christina loved Sultan. She spoke to him, praise and pleasure and nonsense, and he twitched back an ear.

The pines were fenced in with post-and-rails, and a big five-barred gate crossed the track, closed and padlocked. Christina saw it in plenty of time, and gathered Sultan together.

'Come on, you can do that, you splendid beast!'

Sultan pricked his ears, and she knew by the feel of him that he was not afraid. The gate was solid, but he cleared it with plenty to spare, tucking up his hocks. Christina took a pull at him as the trees closed overhead; there were roots running across the path and the pine-needles were slippery, scenting the air with their turpentine smell, mingling with the horse's sweat and the scent of warm leather. He dropped his head obediently, and fell back into an easy swinging trot. It occurred to Christina then that she had left the others a long way behind.

'Steady on, Sultan my boy. We're not being very sociable.'

She turned him round and started to walk back. It was gloomy and strange in the woods, with only the chatter of a squirrel for company. But Christina felt happy in a way she had almost forgotten, with a careless, animal pleasure. No doubts, no disturbing emotions to quell or hide, just sensual content in the feel, the smell, the undemanding company. Sultan went without fuss on a long rein.

When she got back to the gate the others were pulled up on the other side. Sandy had dismounted and was examining the padlock.

'It's jump or nothing,' he said. 'This won't open.'

Dorothy looked at Christina, and Christina saw her annoyance at being at a disadvantage. It pleased Christina enormously.

Will laughed. 'Come on, Christina, jump back again. We're not joining you over there. Unless you want to go solo.'

'An exhibition flight, please,' Sandy said, leading his horse out of the way.

Christina turned Sultan back and trotted him sharply away, praying that he would perform in cold blood as well as he had during the lovely gallop. He came round on his haunches, prancing a little, throwing up his head. Christina hadn't wanted to show off, but her impetuosity had caught up with her. He was, after all, a strange horse to her, and the jump was high. She put him into a canter, her eyes on the top bar. She had jumped far more difficult places than this, but usually with hounds running, when the horse had been as frantic as she to be on the other side. Sultan was suspicious this time; she could feel his slight hesitation, and doubt. She sat down hard, and pressed him on with all her determination. He lengthened his stride, and jumped cleanly, and Christina knew that they understood each other, Sultan and she. She pulled him up in a swirl of sand, and stroked his hot shoulder.

'Excellent!' Sandy shouted. 'Good enough for Hendon—all you want is a good manager!'

Christina swung round and kept Sultan at Will's side as they trotted away through the scrumpled bracken along the side of the ridge. The blue hills of Surrey stood out in the autumn sun, laced with smoky-brown trees and dark rolling acres of heather. It was what Will and Sandy called terrible flying country, and Christina, on her horse, thought even then how strange to ride a steed so ready to let you down with heart failure, that when you were galloping aloft you had to have an eye all the time to a landing place to save your life. She warmed to the bold, reliable horse beneath her seat. She glanced at Will with the old familiar feeling of dread. He looked so easy and safe on the grey mare, his hair blowing back, his fingers sympathetic on the reins. If only this had satisfied his capricious nature, as it had Mark's . . . if only this lovely afternoon had not been—as Christina knew it was— doomed to remaining unique . . . she knew then that she would never ride with him again.

The same evening, when Will took a pupil up just before dusk, the Blériot's engine failed and, in trying to land in the only available space, a clearing full of rabbit-holes in a thick valley full of trees, he turned the Blériot over. The pupil was concussed, and Will broke three ribs.

Christina folded her habit away in the tin trunk, and knew she was back to normal.

CHAPTER 12

Will's accident did not stop him from working. With Joe's help, he had the Blériot in flying order again three days later, and he made no plans to cancel his next exhibition flight, two week-ends ahead.

'What, and lose all that lovely money?' he said to Christina, aghast at the idea. 'It only troubles me when I laugh.'

This was not strictly true, as Christina noticed when she spent her next free afternoon working with him on the Dermot, but she did not argue. She knew how badly he wanted the money. The fact was that by Christmas there were only two or three pilots in the country who were prepared to emulate Pégoud, and Will, being one of them, wanted to exploit his singularity. Christina— stupidly, as she later realized—was surprised. She said to Sandy, 'Why doesn't everyone do it, if it's such an easy way to earn money?'

Sandy looked at her pityingly. 'Why didn't we all jump that gate, when you jumped it on that man-eater? Because we were afraid to try it. It was too difficult. Does that answer your question?'

'You mean Will is a better pilot than most other people?'

'Will is a superlative pilot.'

'Oh.'

It seemed obvious, now Sandy pointed it out, but it came as a slight shock to her. She watched his second exhibition, and acknowledged the truth of it. When he got out of the cockpit after landing, he was besieged by admirers, and lots of girls wrote their names on *Emma*'s fabric, many decorating them with hearts, which made him very annoyed when he surveyed the damage later. There was a picture of *Emma* upside-down in the newspapers, and Will received a flood of invitations from all over the country to repeat his performance. Mr. Adams was very pleased, and ordered a second Blériot with an eighty-horse engine.

'There, you've really touched his granite heart, if he's prepared to shell out a thousand pounds for a new machine,' Sandy said.

Will laughed. 'That's for you,' he pointed out. 'He's expecting you to help me wade through these invitations.'

Sandy made a face. 'I'm quite happy the right way up.'

'You know, a *pair* of machines looping would really be something,' Will said thoughtfully. 'It's worth bearing in mind for the summer.'

Will's success brought a few changes to his life, which pleased Christina. He gave up living in *Emma*'s shed and moved into digs with Sandy in a comfortable house not far from Elm Park. They shared a cluttered but cheerful room overlooking a tidy residential neighbourhood, with a motherly landlady on the floor below, who washed their shirts and did their cooking and generally kept them in order. Christina and Dorothy were invited round once a week for meals, and the domesticity of the scene delighted Christina. Her own room in 'The Bunch of Grapes' was just a dormitory, but this was a home. She loved making toast in front of the fire with Will and Sandy sprawled in the armchairs and Dorothy laying the table, the kettle sizzling on a popping gas-ring, and Sandy's gramophone playing their favourite rag-time.

'Wasting time,' Will called it, thinking of his Dermot.

'Oh, you!' Christina was exasperated.

'How gallant he is!' Dorothy mocked. 'You should get another boy-friend. He'd change his tune then!'

Christina saw the shadow pass over Sandy's face. She put her hand out to him and said, 'All right. Sandy will take me out, won't you, Sandy?'

'Any time you wish, my sweet.'

'Sandy's my friend,' Will said comfortably. 'He wouldn't do that to me.'

There was a knock on the door of the room, and he turned his head and shouted, 'Come in!'

The landlady put her head round and said, 'There's a gentleman asking for you, Mr. Russell. Shall I send him up?'

'Yes, please.'

'It'll be Freddie, I suppose,' Sandy said. 'Better get another cup and saucer out, girls.'

But it wasn't Freddie. Christina, looking up from the hearth, dropped the butter-dish on the tiles with a crack.

'*Mark*!'

Will flung her a startled glance and stood up in one bound.

'Holy Moses! What are you doing here?'

'Just dropped in, if it's convenient,' Mark said, hesitating in the doorway.

Christina found she was gaping like an idiot. She scrambled up, her face flushed with the fire, and Will managed to compose himself enough to say, 'Why, yes, of course, come in.'

He pushed back his chair and went towards Mark with a sudden smile. He held out his hand and Mark shook it, grinning with his old amiable charm. He had not changed at all. His presence was still marked by the restless vitality that Christina had sensed the first time she had met him. It was as if three people had come into the room. The biggest shock of all was that Mark was in army uniform.

'Oh, Mark, this is Miss Saunders—er, Dorothy. And Sandy, Sandy Hardcastle. This is my brother, Mark.' Will made the introductions and they all shook hands. Christina noticed Dorothy's eyes widen with a flush of pleasure as Mark took her hand and looked at her. The way he looked at girls had not changed at all. Christina found herself almost laughing. Then Mark turned to her, smiling, and kissed her on the mouth.

'Christina, how lovely to see you again!'

'Mark!' she said. 'What a surprise!' For some reason, she found she was blushing furiously.

'What on earth's all this?' Will was saying. 'Since when have you been in the army?'

'Oh, I joined up after Christmas. They gave me a commission in the Yeomanry, and I've got Treasure with me. I wasn't sure if the life would suit him, but he seems to have settled all right. I got a bit fed up at home. I was going to join up when the hunting season was over anyway, but young Allington decided to go, and

I thought I might as well too. Father's pretty miserable company these days. He was furious, of course—at least, that I went in the middle of the season. I don't think he'd have minded if I waited till after the point-to-point. Anyway, I'm still going to run Treasure in the point-to-point—he won it last year, Christina. I meant to write and tell you, but I'm not much of a letter writer. Peter Lucas has enlisted too—you didn't know?'

'No,' Will said.

'I suppose you'd go for the Royal Flying Corps, if that's what they call it? If anything blows up, I mean?'

'Yes, Sandy and I have discussed it a few times. I certainly wouldn't join the cavalry.'

'No, by God, they wouldn't have you,' Mark said happily. 'I've been at Aldershot on a course, and I thought I'd pay you a call. I saw a photo in the newspaper—something about some antics at Hendon. There was this photo of an aeroplane upside-down. Was it you, or some chap with the same name?'

'No, it was Will,' Christina said.

'Looks damned dangerous to me. I say, am I butting in, or is it all right? I can't stay long anyway—'

'We're just going to have tea,' Dorothy said. 'Of course you must stay. I've laid another place.'

Christina picked up the butter-dish from the hearth and continued buttering her pieces of toast, still shaken. Why, she thought, spreading furiously, did you expect people to change when you hadn't seen them for a year or two? And then to find nothing was different, only a set of clothes . . . it came as a shock. Mark, in spite of the uniform, was the same animal: easy, quick, aggressive, with the old charm that Christina found even now rubbing off on her. He could be so amiable a companion when he chose, and so brutal and infuriating when he didn't choose. She remembered him vividly in all his moods; he was an open book compared to the withdrawn Will. The last time she had seen him he had proposed to her. Now, over the tea-table, his attitude towards her was familiar and easy, and Christina could sense Will's gradual withdrawal. Of course, she told herself, it was always like this. Will had never committed himself before either his brother or his father. He had always sat at the dinner-table in silence, and any conversations between the two brothers had been brief and generally scornful. Now, after the first quick shock and exchange, the same old habits were taking over. Christina could see the antagonism in Will's dark glances. She could also sense Sandy's fascination, comparing the two brothers, noticing the superficial similarity in their looks and the fundamental division which went so much deeper. And Dorothy, as was to be expected, was fascinated by Mark's vital personality, her golden-brown eyes unable to veil her admiration. Christina, feeling the various reactions to Mark's presence taking place all around her, was aware that she could alter nothing. She felt relieved when Mark re-affirmed that he could not stay long.

'I've got to be back in Aldershot camp at nine.' He pushed his chair back. 'I'd like to see you doing this clever stuff in an aeroplane, Will. When are you performing again?'

'Sunday week,' Will said stiffly.

'I'll see if I can get a pass then, and come over. You must be making money on a lark like that.'

'Yes, I'll be able to pay you the fifty pounds you lost on that wager the time *Emma* frightened the horses.' This was a debt Christina had completely forgotten. Mark laughed. He hadn't.

'Good. I could do with that. I'll keep you to it. Am I seeing things, or does your leg bend these days?'

Will explained about the leg. Mark was impressed. 'These foreign chaps know their jobs, eh? Pity we couldn't get someone like that to do something for Father.'

'How is he?' Christina asked.

'Oh, going down the drain these days. His temper doesn't improve. I don't think anyone could help him now. I suppose you're waiting for him to die so you can get married?' He grinned at Will at the same time as making this outrageous, but deadly accurate, remark.

'Yes,' Will said.

'Well, I don't blame you, considering all you ever got off him was thrashings.' Mark reached for his cap and gloves. 'I'll push off then. See you at Hendon on Sunday week, with a bit of luck.'

131

'We'll be driving over from here in Sandy's motor-car,' Dorothy put in. 'There'll be room for you if you'd like to come.'

'Yes, if you'd like to,' Sandy confirmed politely.

'Oh, very well. Yes.'

'Twelve o'clock, say,' Sandy said.

'Thank you. I hope I can make it.'

'We'll make it a foursome,' Dorothy said pointedly.

Will went down with Mark to see him off. As soon as the door closed behind them, Dorothy turned to Christina, her face alight with malicious enjoyment.

'After what we were saying!' she said. 'You should have seen Will's face when Mark kissed you! Oh, this is splendid! A gorgeous escort like that straight out of the blue—'

Sandy, amused, interrupted, 'You little she-cat!'

'He *is* my cousin,' Christina said coolly, annoyed at Dorothy's machinations. 'There's nothing—'

'So is Will your cousin! I haven't noticed it makes much difference.'

Dorothy could be infuriating at times. Will was very quiet for the rest of the evening, and Christina felt disturbed by meeting Mark again, and having the old family bitternesses revived in her mind. The following Sunday, when she met Will for tea at the Elm Park café, he pushed a small packet over the table towards her.

'I've got something for you,' he said. He had been working on the Dermot all day, and was tired and dirty. Christina took the packet curiously. She opened it and found a velvet ring-box. Inside was a ring of three sapphires mounted in gold, and surrounded with tiny pearls.

'I thought you'd like sapphires best—the colour of the sky,' he explained. He smiled suddenly. 'I couldn't afford diamonds. Not yet.'

'Will!' Christina felt more like bursting into tears than anything else. Her voice wobbled, and she bent her head, pulling off her glove. The ring fitted her finger beautifully.

'We'll be married the day you're twenty-one, or as soon as my father dies, whichever is first,' Will said. 'We'll be all right now. By the summer I shall have paid all my debts, and the Dermot will be finished. I shall take the Dermot to Farnborough, and if it turns out as I'm hoping, I shall get a job designing.'

'No more exhibitions?'

'No, idiot-girl. Don't you see, they are only for money? I don't *like* doing it—it seems quite pointless to me. Hardly any of the spectators appreciate what you're doing—the things they think clever are generally quite easy to do and the difficult bits they don't even notice. It's not like doing it yourself, to find something out, or to test the machine in a particular way, when it all makes sense. Besides, by the middle of the summer, everyone will be looping. A kid of eighteen looped an old Farman last week. Mind you, he couldn't do it again and live, I dare say—' Will grinned at her, and Christina, looking at her ring, remembered the man who had been killed giving an exhibition at Hendon in January, and the nearly-fatal accident the next day of the man the newspapers called the most brilliant of all the instructors. During March a pilot had been killed coming out of a steep dive and tearing the wings off his machine, two were killed when the rudder fell off at three hundred feet, and another killed when he stalled his machine coming into land. Christina remembered all these things for a moment, listening to Will, and smiled.

'It's a lovely ring!'

When Dorothy saw it, her eyes lit up with triumph. 'There, what did I say? It's so that Mark will see it on Sunday, and be warned off. Christina, darling, you must admit that I was right.'

'It's partly that Will has some money for the first time in his life, too,' Christina said. She could afford to laugh at Dorothy now. She was happy.

'I bet Mark will notice it the moment you take your gloves off!'

Mark did, as they picnicked from their hamper before the Hendon meeting began. He congratulated her with a faint irony that did not escape Christina. 'Of course,' he said, 'if you'd have had any sense you'd have married me. I can't see much future in being married to a fellow that fools around in this sort of game.' He gestured with a ham sandwich towards the field, where a Morane-Saulnier was landing at a dangerously high speed.

Christina was goaded by Mark's casual cruelty. 'The best thing I ever did was prefer Will to you! All you wanted was a house-keeper!'

'At least,' Mark said, 'I had a house.' It was just like old times, sparking at each other.

Sandy chipped in, 'Here comes Will now. Go and tell him we've saved him some sandwiches.'

Sandy was not flying, and had driven them over in his motor-car. He looked uncommonly smart in a dark suit, and Dorothy was dressed in the height of fashion, with an enormous hat loaded with white roses which she had to hold on to most of the time. Will and Sandy had been working out how to do an exhibition together, and Sandy was going to time Will's evolutions with a stop-watch and take note of particular effects as they appeared from the ground, in order to improve the performance. Even in this, the sphere he was inclined to despise, Will was a perfectionist, and had spent a good deal of time working on the showmanship angle of the exhibition.

Will, having flown in on *Emma*, joined them, dressed in his flying overalls. Christina noticed, for the first time, that people in the crowd stared at him and nudged each other, but instead of making her feel proud the singling-out gave her a sinking feeling of dread. It seemed to her unreal that Will, the most reserved of characters, had been thrust into this unnatural role. He greeted them cautiously, but Christina could not tell whether his reserve was because of Mark's presence, or because he was preoccupied with the afternoon's work. When it was time for the exhibition, they went out with him to *Emma*, the stewards letting them through. Will checked over the machine and just before he got in he turned and said to Christina, 'By the way, I'm going to do a tail-slide. Don't think anything's gone wrong.'

'No, all right.' She was grateful for the warning, determined not to let Mark see that she had any doubts for Will's safety. She had had plenty of practice now. She could pretend quite easily that she was not worried, walking back across the short grass as Will took off, not even looking. She watched him do his first loop, extend-ing it on the top so that he travelled the whole length of the field upside-down before diving out, and laughed when Mark made some remark about the ham sandwiches.

'No,' she said, 'this is the really stomach-turning trick coming up now.' And if she shut her eyes when Will did the tail-slide everybody else was too fascinated to notice, and she could follow its course by the screaming protest of the falling machine and the engulfing sigh of the crowd.

'That's what plays havoc with ham sandwiches,' Sandy said, clicking his stop-watch as *Emma* roared down in front of the enclosure.

'A remarkable performance,' somebody said behind Christina. Will was coming in to land, and Christina, smiling happily, accepted the comment for herself. She was learning, growing up, giving nothing away. Her own performance had been every bit as remarkable as Will's.

Mark, she was pleased to note, was visibly impressed.

'My God, and to think he couldn't even get Woodpigeon over the ditch out of the Hall meadows!' he said.

Of course, when it happened, it was through no heroics at Hendon, but in the course of an utterly routine take-off from Elm Park. Will was taking *Emma* to Brooklands, to pick up a fitting he wanted for the Dermot, and her engine failed when she was climbing over the boundary of the field. Christina was working in her office and saw Sandy come in through the door. It was the middle of the afternoon, and he was in his flying-clothes. She knew immediately that something was wrong. 'So this is what it feels like,' she thought instantly. 'Now I am going to find out.' She got up and went out through the flap in the reception counter.

'Look, it's all right,' Sandy said at once. 'Nothing fatal—at least, only as far as *Emma*'s concerned. But you'd better go and see Will. He's in hospital, and raving mad. Go and smooth his fevered brow and all that. *Emma*'s a complete write-off.'

'But what happened?'

Sandy explained. 'Of course he had to get straight down, and there was a row of trees in the way, not to mention a hay-stack and a herd of cows. He didn't have a chance. I've got the Ford outside. I'll run you up there if you like.'

'Oh, thank you. I'll tell Mr. Saunders, and get my hat.'

After the first shock of seeing Sandy, and feeling as if all her blood had turned to water, she now felt quite self-possessed, as if the accident was all part of the day's work. Put her typing away . . . a brief word with Dorothy's father . . . her hat and gloves, and Sandy was holding the motor-car door, and swinging the starting-handle.

'Why is he in hospital then, if he's all right?' she asked as they drove through the market-square.

'Well, we didn't see how he could be all right, considering what happened, and he was a bit dopey when we got him out, so he got carted off as a matter of routine. I mean, he looks a mess —he's lost some teeth and he's all shaken up, but there's nothing else, as far as I know.'

So this, at last, was the day Christina found herself visiting Will in hospital. 'As long as it's not the mortuary,' she thought, as the swing doors whooshed behind them and the hospital smell of ether and antiseptic shut out the summer dust. They were shown to Will's room by a nurse, who said, 'Ten minutes', and left them. Will, lying in stiff, snow-white sheets, was undoubtedly a mess, with swollen, cut lips, black eyes and decorations of sticking-plaster. His front teeth were missing, and the adjoining ones crooked.

'Will—oh, heavens, you poor thing—'

'She's come to give you your ring back,' Sandy said. 'She never could abide men with false teeth—'

'I haven't got—'

'No, but you will have, boy.'

Will gave an angry groan. 'It's not teeth I'm worried about,' he muttered. 'It's my engine.'

'You're lucky you're not suffering from permanent lack of breath,' Sandy pointed out. 'I'll go back and see what I can salvage, but I wouldn't bank on very much if I were you. It's pretty well scattered about.'

'I'd rather it was *Emma* scattered about than Will,' Christina said decidedly. 'Ugh, what a scare! Don't do this often, Will, please.' She felt shaky all of a sudden, and sat on the bed, reaching for his hand.

'It's all right,' he said. 'Only my beauty—' He gave her hand a reassuring squeeze.

'Like Mark, when Sweetbriar trod on him.'

'Yes. Not much to spoil . . . We'll have to get that Dermot finished in double-quick time now. I shall have to fly the Blériot on Sunday.'

The instinctive protest rose to Christina's lips, but she cut it off. He was flying the Blériot on Sunday, his face still adorned with sticking-plaster, and Christina thought how strange it was in this

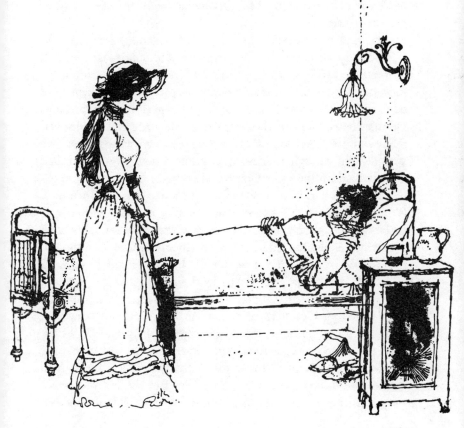

137

irreverent circle that such a near escape from death should pro-
voke not awe, but genuine amusement. Will's lack of teeth—for
the crooked ones had had to come out too—was a particular cause
for hilarity. He stood it nobly—'Wait till I get my new ones—
you won't know me from a movie-star,'—but afterwards he said
to Christina, as if he had only just thought about it, 'If it's so funny
you don't mind, do you? I never thought—'

'They were nice teeth,' Christina said. 'But there's more to you
than just teeth.'

'I mean, if you had no teeth, it wouldn't make any difference to
me.'

'Thank you,' Christina said.

Will saw the funny side then, and laughed. In fact, his lack of
teeth was not unattractive. Christina considered the effect boyish,
rather than ageing.

As spring slipped into summer, Will worked harder than ever.
With Sandy, he perfected the stunting performance that they had
worked out together on the identical Blériots. It was a resounding
success, and they had more invitations to perform than they could
cope with. After the despair of losing *Emma* and the precious
Gnome rotary, Will worked out that by the time the Dermot was
ready—and he had less and less time to spend working on her—he
would have enough money to buy her a new engine. He had
already paid off the Herr Doktor. He bought Christina some expensive clothes to wear at Hendon, and a hat to rival Dorothy's.
It seemed then to Christina that the sun, shining with a rare
enthusiasm that summer, was shining particularly for them, that
everything Will touched now was charmed. Perhaps, she thought,
it was only by comparison with what had gone before—and no
one could deny that Will had had a desperately hard time to get
where he was—but there was a kind of radiance about the time
they spent together that made it seem like something out of a
fairy-tale. Sometimes she thought it was the danger in Will's life
that heightened the pleasure. Sometimes she thought it was the
whole atmosphere of that magical summer, for everyone seemed
touched with the same carefree happiness. Everywhere they went
they had friends. Even the granite-hearted Mr. Adams rejoiced

138

in their success, and the money he was making out of them.

Whether she had genuinely learned not to be afraid, or whether she had merely learned a trick of numbing her feelings and turning her attention away when Will performed the more risky parts of his repertoire, Christina did not try to analyse. She had learned to live with it, whatever it was, and after this summer it would be over. But after this summer there would still remain the growing problem of controlling her feelings, not of fear, but of passion. It did not help, this happiness, these long summer evenings, when suddenly everything was going right for them, to resist the new and terrifying longings. There was no one to advise her. Dorothy was far from being a practical guide in such matters. Such innocence amused her. 'You'll just have to get married, or—' She opened her eyes very wide, and laughed. Christina was nineteen. The next two years stretched out like infinity.

But at the end of June, on the very day the new Gnome rotary was delivered for the Dermot, Will received a telegram from Mark. It said, 'Father dead. Funeral Friday, twelve noon.'

'Thank heavens,' Will said. 'We can get married.'

CHAPTER 13

Will refused to go to his father's funeral. Christina was shocked.

'But Will, you must!'

'Why must I?' Will asked coldly. 'I'm glad he's dead. And I want to put my engine in.'

Christina knew that it was useless to argue. He had cried for Mr. Dermot, but merely shrugged for his father.

Christina bought a black hat and coat and travelled up to London early on the morning of the funeral. There she met Aunt Grace and Aunt Maggie and went on by train with them to Essex. They were met at the local station by Fowler, the groom, driving the carriage and pair. The meeting with old Fowler, who had worked at Flambards all his life, and had even taught Aunt Grace to ride, let alone Christina, was very emotional. Fowler could not see the road for tears, but the horses did not need his guidance. Christina set her teeth, determined not to be caught up in this heart-rending nostalgia, but it was impossible. All her own memories, turning into the Flambards drive and seeing the decayed old house again and the wild garden flaunting its tumbled roses in the sunshine, quite overwhelmed her. She half-expected to see Dick waiting for her with Sweetbriar, his blond hair pale against the weather-beaten brown of his neck, his slow smile greeting her. She remembered her uncle lurching in the doorway on his crutches, burnt up with drink and pain; Mark careless with the foxhounds at his heels, whistling on some errand to the stables; Will shut up in his room out of old Russell's reach, poring over his aerodynamics. But only Mark and Mary, the housekeeper, were waiting in the hall. Russell was in the coffin, propped on trestles, ready for the hearse. Nobody, Christina thought, passed away with less regret than her uncle. Only Mark was genuinely

140

moved, and the elderly servants, Mary and Fowler, were overcome by the occasion more than by any love they bore for Russsell.

'Why, Mark is Russell all over again,' Aunt Maggie said to Aunt Grace, the moment she set eyes on him. (Even to his own sisters, Russell had always been known by his surname.) Christina could not get used to Mark in his Lieutenant's uniform, especially in the familiar Flambards surroundings. He greeted his aunts with a formal embrace, but kissed Christina with a warmth from which she turned abruptly away.

'Where's Will?' he asked.

'He wouldn't come.'

Mark was angry. 'The old man can't hurt him now,' he said with a jerk of his head towards the coffin.

'He just didn't care enough.'

Fair, even in his disapproval, Mark said, 'Well, I can't really blame him.' Everyone else was shocked.

There were a lot of people at the funeral. All the hunting people and the local farmers turned up, and most of the village population crowded the churchyard, agog to see the proceedings. Afterwards there was what amounted to a party at Flambards, where Mary had organized enough drink and meat pie to satisfy the appetites of the hardest horsemen. Christina was relieved when it was time to go, wrenched by meeting all these familiar faces again. Mark was staying on to tidy up his father's affairs, and saw her into the carriage.

'What are you going to do with—with Flambards, and Mary and Fowler? You've got to see that the people are all right,' Christina said, suddenly afraid at the idea of the helpless servants being treated the same way as—long ago, it seemed now—Dick had been.

'Yes, of course,' Mark said, mellow now, and rather drunk. 'They'll stay here and look after the old place.'

They all knew that Mark had been left everything, and William nothing. 'The debts as well,' as Will pointed out later. 'He's welcome.'

Christina was very relieved to get back to Kingston, feeling as if she had stepped back for a day into another century. When she next saw Will, he did not even inquire after the funeral.

'I've been looking up dates,' he said. 'And I think the best would be the Saturday after August Bank Holiday. I'm flying every week-end up till then. That would be the eighth. By then

the Dermot will have shown her paces and—if everything goes according to plan—with luck I'll have got a job somewhere designing.'

'You mean the date for the wedding?' Christina said, wanting to get it right.

'Of course.'

Christina was still attuned to funerals. This time last year it had been Mr. Dermot. She had folded her black away in the trunk, but her feelings would not be so easily put away. She was in the boys' flat; Sandy was having a bath, and for a few minutes she and Will were alone. It was dusk, and warm, yet a soft rain was falling and the room was full of the smell of damp earth coming in through the open windows. Instead of feeling wonderfully happy at the talk of weddings, she felt inconceivably sad. August seemed moons away, with so many days between which suddenly seemed full of traps and dangers. It had been difficult for so long, she could not believe that it was all going to fall into place, merely by their pencilling dates on a calendar. She looked down at the ring on her finger, at the stones the colour of the sky, and started to cry.

'What is it?' Will said, amazed.

Christina could not tell him. She did not know. It was the cold breath that came with the rain, blowing out her courage.

'I want it so,' she whispered, as he put his arms round her. 'Oh, I want it!'

'Christina, sweetheart, don't. Everything is all right now. It won't be long.'

But Christina knew that it would be for ever, this black fear, while she loved Will. She had thought she had it tamed, but now, with a touch of summer rain, it breathed again. Even if she recognized it—and it was so subtle and stifled and tangled a fear, scarcely to be put into words—she knew it was something she must not admit. She had come too far now.

'It's a goose walking over my grave.'

'Oh, graves—!' He stroked her cheek, wiping away the tears. He understood, perhaps, just at that moment. Christina lifted her head so that he could kiss her.

' 'Ere, 'ere, 'ere! What's going on?' Sandy flung a wet towel at the back of Will's head. 'I'll go out and come in again louder. A bit of tact is all that is required.' He slammed the door several times, and thumped across the floor.

'You'll get us thrown out of here, behaving like that,' Will said, with great dignity.

'Hark who's talking! Come and kiss me, Christina. I'm all clean and lovely. Will smells like an oil sump.'

'Yes, he does rather.'

'Well, if the geyser's still working after your attack on it—

which I doubt—I'll go and get all clean and lovely too. I was just telling Christina what day we'd worked out for the wedding, and what does she do? Burst into tears.' Will could see that Sandy had noticed Christina's wet face.

'Quite honestly, I can understand. You'll just have to grin and bear it, Christina. Living with Will is awful, but they say the human being can adjust to anything, given time.'

Will went off to the bathroom, and Christina concentrated on filling the kettle and lighting the gas-ring. She felt better, eased by Sandy's irreverence. He was rummaging in the chest of drawers for some socks without holes, his reddish hair curled with the damp.

'Your Will's happy,' he said. 'He's going to fly his machine tomorrow. Everyone's dying to see if it's going to do all the things he says it will.'

This line of conversation was not calculated to cheer, but Christina could face it, her crust of indifference hardening again by force of habit after its terrible moment of failure. She was ashamed—and Will talking to her of weddings, the thing she most wanted to hear! With almost an eagerness to punish herself, she said, 'Do you think it will?'

'I'll tell you one thing,' Sandy said, pushing his fingers through the toes of yet another sock. 'It won't fall to pieces, whatever else it does or doesn't do. You don't feel like plying a wee darning-needle for a wee moment—?'

'Oh, yes, give them to me.'

'Why don't you come and watch?'

'I'm working tomorrow.'

'What at six o'clock? I'll pick you up in the motor if you like.'

Christina did not commit herself. She did not want to be there, particularly.

'I'll get you back by eight, cross my heart. You ought to be there to see history being made, wave the flag and all that. The first flight of Will's world-beater—'

'Oh, if you promise it won't fall to bits!' Christina caught the socks Sandy threw at her.

'I promise.'

Over supper, Will said, 'About this wedding—' He looked at Christina doubtfully.

'It's all right. I won't cry. I'm resigned to the idea now,' Christina said hastily.

'I saw Aunt Grace, and she's given permission. I had to take a whole evening of unsolicited advice as well, but at least the time spent was not in vain. I thought I could talk her into a civil wedding too, but no—she and Aunt Maggie want the thing done properly, right down to the last carnation.'

'Good. I'm glad,' Christina said.

'Yes. You women are all the same,' Will said darkly.

'Even for you,' Sandy put in, 'Will cannot face wearing a silk topper.'

'As you're going to be the best man, it was you I was thinking of, as a matter of fact,' Will said to him. 'What I wear, you wear too.'

'Oh.' Sandy's face dropped. 'Oh Lord! Shouldn't your brother be the best man?'

'He's got to give Christina away.'

Christina was startled. 'Mark?'

'Who else is there? The only other person is Mr. Saunders, but he's going abroad at the end of July. Mr. Adams I could not face. There's nobody else.'

Christina, suddenly, was amused at the thought of Mark having to give her away. 'He'll be furious!'

'That's his bad luck,' Will said, smiling.

'You'll have to warn him in plenty of time.'

'Yes, that's why I wanted to fix everything with you. So that we can get the banns called, and you'll have to buy some clothes, and there'll be rooms to find, and all that.'

'Oh yes!' Christina was happy now.

'And Sandy's lending us his jalopy for the honeymoon . . .'

Although the talk was of weddings, Christina suspected that Will's air of excitement was in reality due to his being ready to test the new machine, rather than to any wedding plans. This was confirmed in the morning, for when they picked her up at the hotel she noticed at once that Will was very tense and silent. She would gladly have stayed behind, feeling as nervous as Will, but there was no excuse for her. It was a sharp, clear morning, promising heat. Christina wished that it was over.

In spite of its being early, there seemed to be a great many people waiting to see the Dermot fly. Christina was surprised. The mechanics had already wheeled it out of its shed, and it stood on the grass, a small but very powerful looking biplane. Even to Christina's eyes it looked quite different from anything else she had seen flying, with its clean, sharp lines and cowled over engine. It seemed bare, to Christina, almost austere, with a minimum of bracing wires and struts, as far in advance of the old school Farman as Sandy's Model T Ford over a pony-trap. She saw Will looking at it, not saying anything, pulling on his helmet, while everyone pressed round eagerly. Then he was in the cockpit, and Sandy was helping to do up his straps, serious for once. When he was ready, Sandy jumped down and went round to swing the propeller.

The rough, strident din of the engine shattered the summer morning, drowning the skylarks and the blackbirds. Christina felt the blast of the slipstream, shivered and turned away. She heard the machine taxiing away across the grass, and the anticipatory stir of the small crowd. Then Sandy's hand on her arm: 'Come on, Christina!' His voice was almost sharp.

The little machine turned at the far end of the field, her clear-doped wings shining in the sunlight, then came back down the runway fast, faster than Christina had ever seen. Her wheels left the ground, and she climbed up into the shimmering sky like a bird released from a cage. She was so sure and so effortless that, for the first time in her life, Christina felt herself genuinely moved by the beauty of a machine, the emotion seeming to sing through her whole body. A quivering buzz of satisfaction and surprise from the onlookers followed her. The machine was high against the thin early sky in a matter of seconds, sending out brilliants as the sun caught her gleaming metalwork. A high, easy turn, and she was coming back over the field, very fast.

'Oh, and he's not trying yet!' Sandy said, his face alight with excitement. Christina, far from turning away now, found herself quivering with pride.

146

After another climb and circle the machine came back over the field in a long, shallow dive. She came in to land very slowly, so that this time Christina was afraid she was going to stall. She found herself holding her breath, almost wincing. But Will brought the biplane down so that she touched like a feather, and stopped almost immediately. Christina knew enough to appreciate that this great range between top speed and low landing speed was something very desirable; she had never seen it demonstrated so remarkably before. Obviously nor had anyone else, for the enthusiasm was enormous. Will, ready to take off again, had to wait and receive his first congratulations. He nodded cheerfully but impatiently, and taxied away once more. This time he took off and climbed steadily until he was out of sight. When he returned he was very high, and used his height to test stalling speed, and behaviour during tight, steeply-banked turns, and almost vertical dives. By the time he came in to land a second time, the unanimous decision of the Elm Park inhabitants was that Will had a winner on his hands.

Amid all the excitement and technical discussion, Will broke away and came across to Christina. He held out his hand and gave her one of his boyish, oily hugs. 'Come on. I'll drive you back to that doss-house of yours.'

He was very happy. She could see the light in his eye, and the whiteness of his handsome new teeth in the bliss of his smile. The same happiness rose up in her, obliterating all the doubts and strange premonitions of the evening before.

'We'll have a motor of our own soon,' he said, handing her into Sandy's Ford. 'Everything,' he said. 'There'll be no stopping us.'

They laughed. Everything they thought of made them laugh. Christina could not believe that she had not wanted to come.

Christina allowed Dorothy to take her to her own dressmaker to get her wedding dress made. She allowed Dorothy to choose the material and the style, although she turned down Dorothy's first choice as too oriental, and refused to show her ankles. 'I will for my going-away clothes, but not for the wedding.' Dorothy's skirts were daring, three inches above the ankle-bone. Christina was afraid Dorothy, as bridesmaid, was bound to look more handsome than herself, but Dorothy was genuinely eager to turn her into a beauty for the occasion, and Christina was touched. 'I know a very good hairdresser. We'll arrange for him to come and do your hair after you're dressed. And you can spend the night with me and leave from my home. There's far more room to lay all the clothes out than at the hotel. Father will arrange the motors.' The wedding was to be in the Parish church, and the reception at 'The Bunch of Grapes'. Dorothy even made out the invitation lists, and Christina was amazed at all the guests she thought of. Christina, completely ignorant of all the etiquette and procedure that Dorothy took for granted, was awed and grateful for this competent handling of her affairs.

'I've made an appointment for Will and Sandy at the tailor's too. And Will has written to tell Mark about giving you away. There isn't a great deal of time.'

Dorothy was not alone in thinking this. Will was still perfecting the Dermot, having arranged to take it to Farnborough for tests at the Royal Aircraft Factory only ten days before the wedding. He was still doing exhibitions with Sandy several days a week and at Hendon every week-end. Christina longed for all this frenzy to be over, even the wedding. She wanted to be driving away on her honeymoon in Sandy's Model T which he had nobly offered to lend them, with Will at her side, laughing as they had laughed after the first flight of the Dermot.

She knew that Dorothy was looking forward to the wedding, because she would meet Mark again.

'Men look so gorgeous in uniform,' she said dreamily. 'That's what I told Sandy when he was talking about joining the R.F.C. I told him I was mad for him to join.'

'When was he talking about joining the R.F.C.?' Christina asked, curious.

'They both were, last night,' Dorothy said.

'Both? Who do you mean?'

'Sandy and Will, of course.'

Christina tried not to show any surprise, but she felt almost as if Dorothy had hit her.

'Because of this ultimatum to Serbia, you mean? Or is it to do with Ireland? Is that what made them talk about it?'

'Yes, I think so. Trouble—everywhere.' Dorothy was obviously not troubled. 'They both said they would join the R.F.C. if there was trouble.'

Christina, completely involved in her own affairs, had become so used to the background of troublesome politics, like everyone else, that she had not given it more than a passing interest. The Austrian ultimatum to Serbia, she understood, after the shooting of the Austrian Archduke Ferdinand in Sarajevo, was a little more sinister than anything else that had happened in Europe for some time and a great deal of talk was going on about it in Parliament. But worse trouble had been going on in Ireland. Christina found it hard to follow. Will, she thought, understood it, but never spoke of such things. Not since the day, more than two years ago, when they had run away, and he had agreed with Mark's suggestion that there was not much time. Mark had said there was going to be a war.

It was a Friday evening when Dorothy told her this. 'A fortnight tomorrow I shall be married,' Christina thought. In this aura of orange blossom and satin, she thought everything was coming right for her, like the orphans in the fairy-tales. This talk of Dorothy's quivered her careful optimism on its foundations. She read the newspapers the next morning, but it all seemed as meaningless and hysterical as usual. Taking up as much space was an advertisement for the week-end's jaunting at Hendon, with a list of the races and competitions, and Will and Sandy's Sunday stunting in big type.

'It's just talk again,' she thought. 'It will all come to nothing. I am stupid—a born worrier.'

She thought this again on Sunday, when Will and Sandy were making some alterations to their very tightly worked-out performance. Will had been asked to do a tail-slide, and agreed, although Christina knew he did not like doing them because they made him feel sick. She was annoyed that he was too feeble to refuse, and was going to say something sharp; then she remembered that she did not worry. It was no concern of hers if Will wanted to take these unpleasant antics upon himself. She had noticed, and not remarked upon, the fact that the manoeuvres were now done at a height which left the narrowest margin of safety in the event of anything going wrong, and occasionally none at all. But she had watched, and not turned away.

It was a hot, normal, cheerful Sunday, with a record crowd out to enjoy themselves, and Christina forgot the newspapers. Freddie Pugh and his fiancée, a pretty debutante called Emily Appledore, joined them in the enclosure.

'Where's Dorothy today?' Freddie asked.

Christina had a strong suspicion that she had gone out to Aldershot to meet Mark, but Sandy said she was out with relatives.

'So tomorrow's the great day?' Freddie said to Will.

Will grinned. 'Yes, rather. Keep your fingers crossed for me.'

'Surely the wedding is on Saturday week?' Emily said, puzzled. 'The eighth? I've replied to the invitation—'

'The great day they are referring to is the day that Will goes to Farnborough to put the Dermot through her trials,' Christina explained. 'It doesn't refer to the wedding.'

They all laughed, Freddie rather apologetically. Will said, 'You can keep your fingers crossed for that too. More so, if you like.'

'You know where you are with machines,' Sandy said. 'Women are a different matter.'

They strolled across the enclosure, as it was nearly time for the display. The two Blériots stood on the grass side by side. Will did not use the Dermot for this work, as he realized that the use of the identical machines, painted red and silver, improved the look of the figures that were performed in formation. The Dermot had executed every evolution that Will was accustomed to doing in the Blériot, and more, but had not yet performed at Hendon, other than to show her paces. Crowds of admirers thronged round them as they went out on to the field and Christina dropped back, holding on to her hat. She was used to this trampling enthusiasm now, and generally let Will and Sandy get on with it alone, until the stewards came to extricate them.

In the crush she lost Freddie and Emily. It was hopeless looking for them, so she retreated and climbed up into one of the judges' boxes to get a good viewpoint. The officials knew her, and she was allowed to take such liberties. There was an old cane chair in it which she sank into thankfully, for it was very hot. 'Bumpy,' she thought instinctively, as the two monoplanes taxied out across the field—but that was for Will and Sandy to bother about.

She rarely watched the exhibitions by herself, and did not like doing so, for the company of friends, chatting and passing remarks —even making the inevitable jokes about the effects of looping upon the digestion—helped to blanket her own feelings. It was worse now the two machines performed together, for they looped very close together, and Christina knew that Will and Sandy had to watch each other very carefully the whole time. This type of flying had never been attempted before, and was a great attraction to everyone save Christina. After the Dermot, she could not help thinking how very frail the Blériots looked, and wondering how Will's machine could possibly survive a tail-slide, which she had heard him say made it rattle loud enough to deafen him.

She glanced at the clock on the stands. It was three o'clock. In less than ten minutes it would be over. She looked for Freddie and Emily, but could not see them. The crowd below her held up white faces like a field of daisies, making the peculiar rising hum of excitement to which she had grown so accustomed. Then the hum dropped to a dead silence, which made her feel cold, and very lonely, and, like some stricken bird from the upper atmosphere, Will's machine came plunging down in the spectacularly horrible tail-slide, howling in protest, silver wings splayed out, whipping between the straining wires. Down, down—Christina wanted to scream with it, feeling the sweat rise and the pulses race. Alone, the panic grasped her and squeezed her. This is what she could master when she was with friends, even just with Dorothy. But alone in her isolated box, she stuffed her gloved hands up to her mouth, frightened she would cry out.

The Blériot came out of the tail-dive with the ghastly lurch that strained every splinter of its fabric, and brought up Will's dinner. As it tipped over into the ensuing nose-dive, the crowd gave its great sigh, that came up to Christina like a chorus elicited by some invisible conductor. Unexpectedly the machine came out of its nose-dive and immediately did a loop, pulling out lower than Christina had ever seen, and the chorus swelled up into a crescendo of delight upon which the gleaming silver wings seemed to be lifted again, zooming up against the cloudless sky. 'Oh, you fool!' Christina whispered, but she was enchanted too, and full of a wonderful, laughing pride, as strong as the fear. At last she found she could breathe again. She glanced at the clock, smoothed the wrists of her gloves, and adjusted the pink silk rose on the collar of her dress, glad that no one had seen her make a fool of herself. The two machines were out of her sight over the roofs of the stands, joining up to do their finale, a simple but very effective display of vertical banking, going round the field in opposite directions. They missed each other with what looked like hair-raising casualness, but which was in fact extremely well-rehearsed precision. The crowd loved this. Looking down, Christina caught sight of Freddie and Emily near the rails below her box, and decided to join them. She bent down and picked up her bead bag which had slipped off the chair on to the floor. She heard the crowd give a roar of delight, and saw one of the machines come skimming low in front of the enclosure. Beyond it, the other had zoomed up on the other side of the field, coming round to meet it again. But at the top of the bank, it gave an unexpected jerk, and started to go into a sideslip. It was at about a hundred feet, and went down with a scream of wires that Christina could hear from her box. The crowd went silent instantly, and into that silence the impact as the machine hit the ground exploded with a sickening clarity. Christina heard the splintering of wood and steel, the crack of hot splitting metal and saw the shower of debris and dust and turf go up as if a great hammer had pounded the dry earth. She also saw quite clearly in her mind the simultaneous end of the human body, as frail in its final predicament as the machine itself. She knew immediately that what she saw was final; it was death, not a question of missing teeth or sore ribs.

The incident was as quick and clean and decisive as one of the tricks that had preceded it. It was almost as if, for a moment, the

crowd did not apprehend that this was not in the repertoire, for the silence was like a livid strangulation of breath across the whole length of the enclosures, broken only by the distant noise of the surviving Blériot. Christina, looking down from her perch, saw a spearhead break out of the crowd and start to run across the field. Led by white-clad officials it moved, apparently slowly, across the green turf like lava. She watched it, frozen and quite unable to move. A crash tender converged from the other side, more nimble than the crowd, and she went on watching as if it were very important to see what happened. But she knew that whatever the helpers did, to help in any way that mattered was beyond their powers.

The other Blériot, continuing its circle, flew over the scene, coming low over the smoking debris. Christina saw the helmeted, anonymous head looking over the side of the fuselage, and did not know whether it was Will taking in Sandy's death, or Sandy taking in Will's. She watched the living pilot in an agony, unable to move her eyes away.

'Christina! Christina, darling!' Emily was running up the steps of the box, her face as white as her dress.

'Who is it?' Christina said instantly.

Emily was crying. 'I don't know! I don't know! Freddie thinks it's—it's—' Emily could not say the name, so that Christina knew, without her saying.

'I must find out,' she said blindly. 'Somebody must know.'

'They went over the stands and turned, and we didn't notice which was which afterwards. Nobody seems to know.'

The other Blériot was landing, but on the far side of the field because of the crowd, too far away to see properly. Christina turned and started to run, half-falling, down the steps. Emily followed her. Christina ran through the milling crowd and out on to the field, her breath jerking in her throat. The grass was hot in the sunshine, smelling of hay and pollen, recently mowed. Christina, as she ran, remembered Mr. Dermot and the buttercups and her dead uncle among the summer roses of Flambards, and the black dress folded away in her trunk. 'It—cannot be—be—' she gasped out to Emily. 'It cannot—' But she had no breath to talk, only to run, the pretty silk dress clutching at her knees, binding her up. She felt her hat go, and her hair slipping. Somebody was getting out of the Blériot, a tall, thin figure—like Will, like Sandy. There were people all round him; he disappeared from her sight, closed in by seething spectators. She got to the edge of the people, and started to push her way through. They seemed to close against her. She thrust at them, and beat at the black-suited shoulders, and they gave way in amazement to her frenzy, falling back. 'Let her through,' they said, recognizing her agony. 'Let her through.' The figure in flying-overalls had his back to her but turned as she came up.

'*Will!*'

Christina flung herself on him, a wild joy going through her that was as painful as it was real. He held her for a moment, long enough for her to contain herself, then she was able to step back, all in hand again, like somebody else. Emily came up, and handed her her hat, in a mute and unlikely gesture that Christina accepted as part of this awful strangeness.

They walked back across the grass together, with all the officials and the crowd round them. Will did not say anything, apart from a few nods and monosyllables to the people who all seemed to have plenty of opinions to pass. He seemed to Christina very much under control, so that she felt bound to explain her hysteria.

'I thought it was you,' she said.

'Yes, I understand.'

The shock on the field had passed into a subdued excitement. The crowd was breaking up, turning away, the lava rolling back, chivvied by police and officials. Alone on the scarred grass, the remains of the silver Blériot lay scattered, still attended by the men off the crash tender, sifting through the bits. Will did not give it another glance. The ambulance had already left. The tidying up was swift and brutal, and very matter-of-fact.

They went into the manager's

office, and someone poured out some brandies. Will refused one, but Christina found a few sips a considerable help. The whole business took on a complete unreality. People kept coming in and out. Christina heard Will discussing the following week-end and heard him say, 'I'll bring the Dermot over and do something with her. Then the next week-end I'm being married. I'm not making any more engagements after that, until I know what I'm doing as regards the Dermot.'

'Yes. Very well. Things are very uncertain just at the moment, in any case.'

Will turned to Christina. 'I'll fly the Blériot back to Elm Park, and you can drive back with Freddie. I'll see you at the flat. Is that all right? Do you mind?'

He looked at her anxiously. 'That's all right,' she said.

She left with Freddie and Emily in his Lanchester tourer at the same moment as Will took off. The crowd had dispersed, and the sun had lost its warmth. Christina watched the Blériot, pulling the motor-wraps round her, shivering a little. The monoplane was all alone now over the empty expanse of the field. She saw it take off over the remains of its companion, then instead of gaining height and heading away for home, it turned and came back over the wreckage again, quite slowly, looking very lonely.

Christina found she was grinding her teeth together, the tears welling up. 'So much for Will's composure,' she thought. For a moment, in her mind, she could see his face as he looked down over the wing at the remains of Sandy's machine. She knew then that he was showing no more restraint than she had shown a little earlier, when she had found who it was that had died.

CHAPTER 14

When they got back to the flat, Will was already there. So were several other people from Elm Park, and some newspaper reporters. The landlady was shuffling through the unaccustomed visitors, crying. The lamps were lit in the first-floor room and, as it was still very warm, the windows were open wide behind the net curtains, which bulged and fell in the draught. Two flypapers swung from the tasselled lampshades. Will lay back in the arm-chair, a glass of whisky in his hand, listening to Freddie and Joe talking across him. 'It could have happened to anybody. It could just as easily have been Will.' 'He didn't have the height to get out of it.' Will did not join in. He had changed into a clean shirt and trousers, and complained about the heat, but did not say anything else. Christina did not want to fuss. He just said to her, with a nod across the room, 'See to them,' and Christina got the glasses and drink out, and set them on the table. She went into the bedroom to put her hair up properly, and saw Sandy's handsome silk pyjamas slung untidily across a chair, and the tatty old coat he wore for motoring, and the shoes with oil all over them, and the socks with the inevitable holes. She concentrated on her hair, desperate to get back into the crowd. 'Don't think about it,' she said to herself. 'Think of something else.'

As the evening went on, the crowd kept changing, but did not disperse. The talk, hushed at first, grew louder, and—because Sandy had been essentially a humorous person—it seemed that everyone could remember one of his funnier stories, or recount one of the joky things that had happened in the old Farman, or while motoring in one of his temperamental vehicles. There was chuckling, and some irresistible bursts of laughter. One of Sandy's old pupils put Sandy's favourite ragtime record on the gramophone and, instead of being shocked, Christina found it oddly comforting, playing quietly into the soft draughts through the windows. 'After all,' as Freddie remarked when he left, 'this is his style, isn't it? Not the old gnashing of teeth and drawing the curtains.'

When there were only a few people left, and it was past midnight, Christina went over to Will.

'What are you going to do tonight? Stay here?' The room seemed to her now as if it were lying in wait, until the numbing buffer of chatter had all gone away, and when they were alone it would overwhelm them utterly. She did not think she could face it. Will got up wearily and shook his head, as if his thoughts were the same as hers. But at that moment Joe, Mr. Dermot's Joe, with his stolid, country tact, came across and said to Will, 'If you'd like to come back to Elm Park with me, sir, you can sleep in my shed tonight. Then you'll be all ready for the morning.'

Will's face cleared. 'Yes, that's a good idea.' He looked at Christina, and put an arm round her shoulders. 'What about you? Will you come too?'

'Yes.'

They got their coats and drove back with Joe in Sandy's own Ford, which Joe had used. The air was cool at last, and the stars were shining. In the shed, with the Dermot gleaming in the thin light that came through the glass panels in the roof, Christina had this feeling of unreality again. Joe put the kettle on to boil, and Will flung himself down on his old bed.

'You use my bed, Miss Christina. I'll roll myself in the tarpaulin,' Joe said.

The situation was ludicrous in the extreme, lying on Joe's truckle bed drinking tea at one in the morning, yet Christina knew that—to Will as well herself—it was the most bearable way to pass this unbearable night. If the circumstances were unthinkable, so was the fact that Sandy did not exist any more. Exhausted, Christina slept, but her dreams woke her, sick and sweating with their closeness. She turned her head and saw Will, lying with his hands clasped behind his head, awake, looking up at the square skylight where the stars were pale now in the dawn. His expres-

sion, unguarded, exposed his feelings utterly. His attitude sharpen-
ed Christina's own pain to the point where she felt she could
not move or speak, or scarcely even breathe, for fear of giving
way to emotions which she knew would swamp her completely.
She had no experience to draw on, she did not know how it was
possible to give comfort, or receive it, in such a situation. She felt
that if she were to make even the smallest gesture towards Will,
the grief would come up like a rogue wave over a small boat and
they would drown together, while Joe snored softly in his tarpaulin. It was not that she had no feelings, that she lay so quietly,
but that the feelings were too wild to be let out. And from the
look on Will's face, she thought he was not very different.

It was not much better in the morning, when the unreality
gave way to cold light of day. There were Sandy's pupils to be
put off, and Will had to get to Farnborough for his trials. He was
out with Joe testing the Dermot at five, and Christina doubted
whether he had slept at all. He came in for his breakfast, and
Christina got his things ready, his gloves, and map, and clean
goggles, like a suburban housewife. No word was mentioned of
the unbelievable thing that had happened. When he was ready to
go, Christina went out to the machine with him (like going to the
garden gate, she thought), and kissed him good-bye.

'You've been marvellous, Christina,' he said, the only hint that
this day was unlike any other. 'I'll call for you when I get back
tonight, and we'll go out to dinner.'

'Yes. Very well. Good luck.'

He flew away, and Christina went back to her office, where it
was just another Monday morning, with a pile of letters to type
out, and extra provisions to order for the forthcoming Bank
Holiday. Dorothy had not yet returned from wherever she had
gone, but no doubt knew of Sandy's death, for the newspapers
were full of it.

In the evening, as he had promised, Will called for her. He
wore a dark suit, very tidy and smart, and Christina had put on a
dress of pale grey *crêpe-de-chine* with the very fashionable new
V neck which Will had bought her only two weeks before. Things
were very different for them since the time Will had taken her

out to dinner after his return from Switzerland. Now the waiter recognized Will and showed them to the best table, and Christina was used to Will being pointed out by other diners, or even being asked for his autograph. But she did not think anyone would ask him for his autograph tonight.

The trials had been the success everyone had predicted.

'It went splendidly. They gave her a climbing rate of twelve hundred feet per minute, a top speed of ninety-five and a stalling speed of thirty-seven. And they offered me a job.'

'In the Royal Aircraft Factory?'

'Yes. Designing.'

'The job you've always wanted?'

'Yes.'

Will was smiling, but there was something guarded in his manner that stopped Christina's instinctive excitement. She looked at him closely.

'It will mean that we shall go there to live then, after the honeymoon? Near Farnborough?'

For a moment, a fleeting ironical moment, she saw Will in a desk, smart and clean as he was now, drawing aeroplanes, happy, fulfilled. She saw him coming home in the evening in a new motorcar to a cottage with roses up the front wall and herself waiting at the gate, the evening dusk overlaid with the pleasant aroma of his dinner cooking. He would get down and kiss her, and he would smell of pencil shavings, not oil, and his beautiful bony fingers would be quite clean, save for a little ink here and there. And at the same time she knew perfectly well that this vision was as unreal as everything else these last twelve hours.

'What is it?' she said.

'There's something else,' Will said. His dark eyes, looking black against the pallor of his fatigue, were regarding her with something she could only recognize as pity. 'I should have told you before—before all this happened, before yesterday—but I was afraid to tell you.' He was still afraid.

There was a long silence between them. Then Christina said quietly, 'I know what it is.'

'Did Dorothy tell you? Sandy and I had both decided.'

'Yes. She told me how gorgeous men look in uniform.'

'Would it be any consolation to you then, me looking gorgeous?'

'No,' she said blindly.

'But you understand that it really isn't a matter of choosing? If this war business comes to anything, it won't just be me?'

'No.' Nor just herself either, Christina supposed coldly. She wasn't the only girl in the world in love. If Will hadn't been so gentle, so kind, it would have helped a lot.

'I said I'd let them know about the job. If everything turns out all right, it's the very thing I've always wanted. But if it doesn't, then I shall enlist in the Royal Flying Corps.'

Christina could see that he was so sad for her, and yet already committed, whatever she was to feel. As if seeing this himself, he said quickly, 'I said it was going to be hard for you, Christina. I didn't know just how bad, then. Things like Sandy—' He paused. 'But if you feel you've had enough, I wouldn't blame you. It's not too late to back out—'

'Why, do you want me to?' Christina could hardly get the words out.

'No. It would be worse than yesterday, ten times worse.'

'Don't say such things then!' Christina, having faced what she had thought was the worst, could not face this. She looked at Will, and saw at once from his face that he couldn't either, and everything fell into place. Everything was quite bearable once more.

She smiled, a little shakily. 'Heavens, the frights you give me!'

'Yes, I'm good at it. That's the trouble.'

'Well, this new one of yours—enlisting, I mean—is not really anything you can help, I understand that.'

She remembered Sandy joking: 'The human being can adjust to anything, given time.' It really was no joke at all. Once she had been afraid of merely rolling across the field on the old Farman. But she had adjusted. She would adjust, given a few more days, to the hole where Sandy had been, and to Will wearing a uniform.

Sandy's funeral was the worst: the smell of roses and carnations in the church, and his suffragette mother crying—and she had not bothered to make him hot dinners, Christina remembered indignantly, but only left him cold meat and salad. Being very progressive, she had chosen cremation instead of a burial. Freddie said with grim humour to Will, 'If he hadn't switched his engine off, he's have got himself cremated for free, and saved her the trouble.' It was a desperate hour for Christina, tightly clutching Will's hand in the hard sanctuary of a high-backed pew, knowing that Sandy's rare attendance at church had been planned for her wedding, not for this. They did not go to the funeral lunch, but raced back home and changed out of the horrible black clothes and drove out into the country and had lunch in a little pub on the Hog's Back. There, curiously, they were happy at last. The beer was cool and pleasant and there was a home-made pie, and a wooden table in a bit of garden where the bees moaned pleasantly in a tumbled bed of flowers. Christina pulled off her hat and shook back her hair, and felt the hot sun like balm.

'Nothing can ever be so bad again,' she said.

'No,' Will agreed. 'It's over.'

They walked up off the road through fields of dozing cows, up on to a chalky brow where there were swarms of little butterflies as blue as the sky itself. Far below, in the village shop a newspaper proclaimed in thick black headlines 'Austria declares War', but Will and Christina did not care any more. It wasn't that Christina had to make any great effort of will-power not to care, but it seemed perfectly natural to be bound up now in this strange excitement that had taken hold of the summer. It was as if all the sorrows and excitements of their own lives were now very small and of no great importance, for what was happening was out of their hands. And—more strange still—it was not sad and terrible that the country was on the brink of going to war, but terrifically thrilling.

'Come on, Mrs. Russell!' Will shouted at her, and they ran down the slope on the other side, leaping and jumping. Christina, breathless with stitch and laughter, thought, 'I can face anything now, anything at all!' and it wasn't just a whim of the moment, because of the sun and the release of forgetting Sandy; it was true.

'I'm not the only one,' she thought again, on Sunday, when

Will was flying the Dermot at Hendon, for the talk was all of enlisting and mobilization. In fact the flying did not seem to be very important. In the evening big crowds surged outside Buckingham Palace, and Christina laughed at Will when he kissed her good night, and said, 'I only love men in uniform! I think they're gorgeous!'

'It's only this darned appointment I've got to keep next Saturday that's holding me up,' Will murmured. 'This wretched girl I've got to marry ...'

'What a nuisance for you!'

'Oh, a lovely, heavenly nuisance ...'

Two days later, Britain declared war on Germany. Will enlisted and received an appointment to go before a Medical Board three days after the end of his honeymoon.

'There,' Dorothy said, 'I think that's fixed it. For heaven's sake don't toss your head, Christina.'

'I'm hardly likely to,' Christina said, very stately before the long mirror in Dorothy's bedroom. The scent of her orange-blossom bouquet was mingled with the sharp smell of hair fresh from the curling tongs. Dorothy had fixed the veil on top of the hairdresser's work, and was very anxious about its survival.

Christina glanced at the gilt-mounted clock by Dorothy's bedside. 'Has Mark arrived yet?'

'Yes. There's a family reunion going on downstairs, Mark and your aunts. The old girls are crying already.'

Christina giggled. 'Poor Mark!'

'You're not at all well off for relatives,' Dorothy remarked, 'And both of you coming from the same family makes it worse. It's very strange to have a wedding with no mothers and fathers at all.'

'There wouldn't be a wedding, if Will still had a father,' Christina pointed out.

'No, true. Parents can be tiresome, I suppose. You look perfect, Christina, if I say it myself. I'm going to take all the credit. Mark will be mad with jealousy, giving you to Will.'

'Not with you standing right beside me,' Christina said,

smiling. Dorothy had wept bitterly for Sandy, but only for the past they had shared, not the future. She had made no secret of her new infatuation. She smiled now, and glanced at herself in the mirror. Her rich auburn beauty made Christina look almost delicate by comparison. But Christina was not afraid of comparisons.

'We'd better go down,' Dorothy said. 'You don't want to keep poor Will waiting. I do hope Freddie got him organized properly. Have we got everything? Have you got a handkerchief, in case you cry?'

'I won't cry,' Christina said.

Never had she felt more sure of any fact, than that.

They went downstairs. Aunt Grace and Aunt Maggie had left, and Mark was chatting to a pretty maid, who was giggling in the hall.

'Jeepers!' he said, raising his eyebrows, and looking from one to the other.

'You're taking the place of Christina's *father* today,' Dorothy said pointedly.

'Not yours though.' Mark's reply was equally pointed, and amused. He held out his arm for Christina. 'Come on, child. Are you happy?'

'Yes.'

It was curious to be able to acknowledge this fact so freely and without any doubt, in spite of everything that had happened. It gave Christina a feeling of great strength. She looked at Mark fondly. There was no doubt that the uniform was rather gorgeous; she saw Mark, and pictured Will, with shining boots and Sam Browne belt and rows of medal ribbons, given time. She was proud and excited, and would not have had it any different.

'You look frightfully smart!'

'I did a bit of extra spit and polish for you—I didn't want to let you down. I wouldn't do it for everyone.'

'For heaven's sake, Mark, be careful if you step back, with those spurs. Remember Christina's train.' Dorothy was taking her duties very seriously.

'Yes, all right. Give me a nudge if I do anything wrong. Your timing was just right, Christina. We're leaving for France on Monday.'

Christina recognized the excitement in his voice, as if it were a point-to-point, or a particularly good day's hunting that he was anticipating. She knew now that life was suddenly dangerous for very many more people than just Will. She would no longer be alone with her fears. In fact, she had the advantage of being proved and tried: she had come through, all calm and collected, to please Will, and now she knew that she had the practice, or the strength, or the courage—whatever it was—to face anything that might happen. She was streets ahead in experience, while all the other girls were only just starting. She could afford to laugh; her confidence was unshakable. (And she had known, in her heart, that the vision of Will in a desk had never stood a chance. Will had never pretended to her, right from the start.)

When they walked out to the Rolls-Royce, shining and be-ribboned in the August sunshine, she remembered the last Rolls-Royce, when Will had driven her away to Aunt Grace's and Mark in his drunken rage had chased them on his grey hunter.

'You should be on Woodpigeon,' she said softly to Mark. It was very cruel, but she could not resist it. And to her great satisfaction Mark smiled and said, very avuncular, 'We've grown up since then.'

'Is that what it is?'

'Of course.'

Christina was enchanted with the explanation, so firm and simple. She wanted no more. She waved happily to the small knot of women and children that had gathered on the pavement to watch, and the Rolls-Royce moved off.

The Eagle of the Ninth
Rosemary Sutcliff
ISBN 0 19 271765 0

The Ninth Legion marched into the mists of northern Britain. And they never came back. Four thousand men disappeared and the Eagle standard was lost. Marcus Aquila, a young Roman officer, needs to find out what happened to his father and the Ninth Legion. He sets out into the unknown territory of the north on a quest so hazardous that no one expects him to return . . .

Outcast
Rosemary Sutcliff
ISBN 0 19 271766 9

Sickness and death came to the tribe. They said it was because of Beric, because he had brought down the Anger of the Gods. The warriors of the tribe cast him out. Alone without friends, family or tribe, Beric faces the dangers of the Roman world.

The Silver Branch
Rosemary Sutcliff
ISBN 0 19 271765 2

Violence and intrigue are undermining Rome's influence in Britain. And in the middle of the unrest, Justin and Flavius uncover a plot to overthrow the Emperor. In fear for their lives, they find themselves leading a tattered band of loyalists into the thick of battle in defence of the honour of Rome.

The Lantern Bearers
Rosemary Sutcliff
Winner of the Carnegie Medal
ISBN 0 19 271763 4

The last of the Roman army have set sail and left Britain for ever. They have abandoned the country to civil war and the threat of Saxon invasion. When his home and all he loves are destroyed, Aquila fights to bring some meaning back into his life, and with it the hope of revenge . . .

The Ship That Flew
Hilda Lewis
ISBN 0 19 271768 5

Peter sees the model ship in the shop window and he wants it more than anything else on earth. But it is no ordinary model. The ship takes Peter and his brother and sisters on magical flights, wherever they ask to go. They fly around the world and back into the past. But how long can you keep a ship that is worth everything in the world, and a bit over . . . ?

Minnow on the Say
Philippa Pearce
ISBN 0 19 271778 2

David couldn't believe his eyes. Wedged by the landing stage at the bottom of the garden was a canoe. The *Minnow*. David traces the canoe's owner, Adam, and they begin a summer of adventures. The *Minnow* takes them on a treasure hunt along the river. But they are not the only people looking for treasure, and soon they are caught in a race against time . . .

Tom's Midnight Garden
Philippa Pearce
Winner of the Carnegie Medal
ISBN 0 19 271793 6 (hardback)
ISBN 0 19 271777 4 (paperback)

Tom has to spend the summer at his aunt's and it seems as if nothing good will ever happen again. Then he hears the grandfather clock strike thirteen—and everything changes. Outside the door is a garden—a garden that shouldn't exist. Are the children there ghosts—or is it Tom who is the ghost?

A Little Lower than the Angels
Geraldine McCaughrean
Winner of the Whitbread Children's Novel Award
ISBN 0 19 271780 4

Gabriel has no idea what the future will hold when he runs away from his apprenticeship with the bad-tempered stonemason. But God Himself, in the shape of playmaster Garvey, has plans for him. He wants Gabriel for his angel . . . But will Gabriel's new life with the travelling players be any more secure? In a world of illusion, people are not always what they seem. Least of all Gabriel.

A Pack of Lies
Geraldine McCaughrean
Winner of the Carnegie Medal and
the Guardian Children's Fiction Award
ISBN 0 19 271788 X

Ailsa's life is turned upside down when a strange man moves into her mother's antique shop. He keeps the customers spellbound with his outrageous stories—adventure, horror, romance, mystery—but Ailsa doesn't believe a word. It's all just a pack of lies . . .

Brother in the Land
Robert Swindells
ISBN 0 19 271785 5

Danny's life will never be the same again. He is one of the unlucky ones. A survivor. One of those who have come through a nuclear holocaust alive. He records the sights and events around him, all the time struggling to keep himself and his brother alive.

Flambards
K. M. Peyton

ISBN 0 19 271783 9

Twelve-year-old Christina is sent to live in a decaying old mansion with her fierce uncle and his two sons. She soon discovers a passion for horses and riding, but she has become part of a strange family. This brooding household is divided by emotional undercurrents and cruelty . . .

This is the first book in the award-winning Flambards series.

Wolf
Gillian Cross
Winner of the Carnegie Medal

ISBN 0 19 271784 7

Cassy hears sinister footsteps in the middle of the night. Suddenly she is packed off to stay with her beautiful, feckless mother. There is no explanation. Something has gone frighteningly wrong.

Danger is coming after Cassy. And behind it lurks the dark wolf-shape that seems to slink into everything.

Even her dreams.

The Great Elephant Chase
Gillian Cross
Winner of The Smarties Prize and the Whitbread Children's Novel Award

ISBN 0 19 271786 3

The elephant changed their lives for ever. Because of the elephant, Tad and Cissie become entangled in a chase across America, by train, by flatboat and steam boat. Close behind is Hannibal Jackson, who is determined to have the elephant for himself. And how do you hide an enormous Indian elephant?

The Hounds of the Morrigan
Pat O'Shea

ISBN 0 19 271773 1

The Great Queen, the Morrigan, is coming from the West, bringing destruction to the world. Only two children can stop her. At times their task seems impossible, and danger is always present. But they are guided in their quest by an unforgettable collection of humorous and joyful characters.

But all the time the Morrigan's hounds are trailing them . . .